Laying WITH THE LADY IN BLUE

URBAN LEGEND EROTICA COLLECTION

HONEY CUMMINGS

4 Horsemen
Publications, Inc.

Dedication

To Erik

I had two pieces to the next trio; Bloody Mary and Woman in White.

Thanks for sharing the alluring ghost story of the Blue lady from Story, Indiana!

XOXO
Honey Cummings

Table of Contents

1

Bed & Breakfast

Jane Story stood in the dark foyer of her old Bed & Breakfast. The building had been built when Story, Indiana was founded in 1851 as a logging community. Later, hippies purchased the place, then re-assembled the whole town as a tourist attraction. At least, it brought the past into the present, and the community was better for it, despite the highways diverting their traffic away. Despite all the changes and the passage of time, the B&B held its own. A relic covered in vines, rust, and still as inviting to visitors as the day it first opened.

Hands on her hips, Jane was a curvy thing in her tight cut-off jeans and light blue crop top. The outfit made her look like a brown-haired model from a clothing ad for high-end stores, where a simple white shirt costed triple the price of a similar thrift shop find. She took pride in being old fashioned, and she loved the old inn with all her soul. On days like this, she wanted to feel alive or at least blend into the current times.

Her hair had been jumbled into a messy bun and she blew a strand from her face as she lit her pipe. An old habit she kept going, though she hadn't seen anyone come through the B&B smoking a pipe in decades. This had always been her one vice, a gift from her beloved husband in fact, and she couldn't part with it. The aromatic cherry tobacco filled the room quickly as she waved the match.

Glancing up, she scowled at the no smoking sign. *Make me,* she thought with a smirk.

Pipe in her lips, she removed her gardening hat and gloves, happy to assist in keeping the old place alive and well. It had been hers for some time, but at last, it had swapped owner-ship multiple times. The latest owner and management seemed to enjoy it's quaint and quirky qualities, quelling her need to quarrel with anyone about it. They had refurbished the rooms in their original design, though modernizing the amenities to encourage pleasant stays for their guests. She hadn't been asked to help, nor did she work there. They simply allowed her to come and go as she pleased, letting guests know she was the former owner and visited from time to time.

The garden is sorted, so now to the next matter. Another col-lege boy is staying the night. Wonder if I can just get by and avoid them altogether. Annoying shit, that business.

Tired from the heat of the day on her bare tan shoulders, she climbed the steps. They had indeed told guests of her coming and going to the point where the local college now made a game out of staying in a room. The college brats took turns, some coming back on multiple occasions, with one goal in mind; see who could lay with the Lady in Blue. She preferred it that way instead of her true namesake, and she'd keep it that way with the rash of blue balls and broken hearts she'd returned to the campus.

A trail of pipe smoke lingered in the air in her wake. Behind the front desk, the receptionist coughed and hacked, waving it from his face. They stared into the darkness with a deep frown, chasing the smoke up the empty stairs.

"There she goes again. I wish she'd stop smoking; it's killing my sinuses." Snuffling his nose, he settled back into his chair. "Now, where was I in this book? Oh, yeah... the jail scene."

Jane wondered the halls, checking each door was locked and secured. One was cracked and she pulled it shut, nice and quiet as not to wake the old couple spending the week at the B&B. Satisfied all was in order, she spun to her room, then paused at the door. Her blue lamp was on, the glow coming through the bottom of the door, casting an eerie glow across the hall carpet.

Who the hell is in my room? Anger filled her and she pulled her pipe from her plump lips. *Don't tell me... I'm going to kill that pukwudgie. This is his doing!*

Pushing through the door, she stopped at the bathroom door, glaring at her bed. Not one, but two college kids were having the time of their life in her sheets, on her quilt, in *her room*. Crossing her arms, she watched them with jealous intrigue. The blonde was naked, her pale skin blue under the lamp's light as she rode atop the man. Her body thin, she was petite compared to Jane. There was a level of admiration though, the way her body waved as she straddled her lover. Torso snaking provocatively as she grinded against the cock she rode.

Athletic arms reached up, cupping her subtle breasts, making her pink nipples more pronounced. Jane's face grew hot as she followed the overlapping layers of muscles back to their owner's face. He bit his bottom lip, his lustful eyes making Jane completely jealous. They both moaned, arching against each other. Sweat painted their bodies, showing how long they'd been at it, neither paying heed to Jane's presence in the room. His caramel skin a sexy contrast against the milk of her slender body. Long black locks of hair stuck to his face, his expression tense and focused.

He muttered between groans, crooning in Spanish. It was enough to even make Jane wish she'd been in the girl's place but shook her head. After all, she had been waging war against the hazing ritual they had rudely made her part of. Until they stopped, she refused to give into their game. Last thing she wanted was her B&B becoming the Blue Lady's Whorehouse. She snorted, thinking about how her belated husband would roll over in his grave if she let their dream home twisted in such a way.

Her eyes fell on the man's lips, thick and plump as they spoke foreign words of lust and love. *Lips like that, he's gotta be a good kisser.*

A phone buzzed on the bathroom vanity, scattering Jane's thoughts. Curious, she picked it up, safely assuming the pink glittery case belonged to the blonde harlot shrieking in pleasure. She unlocked the phone and read the text. If they were going to invade her space, she would do the same, in the only means she had: *their phones.*

[Mark: Hey Babe. Where u at?]

Oh? Another man is looking for her. She's a busy one.

From the room, she heard the girl mutter, "Phillipe! Oh, oh, harder baby. Deeper... y-yes..."

Another wave of Spanish and moaning came from her partner. Jane rolled her eyes.

She dove into the string of texts between this Karen and Phillipe. There, she found sexting and fanned herself. She didn't need to watch them anymore. *Jackpot!* She had found a trove of dick pics and sultry pics exchanged between the two.

The size of that man's cock! Another shriek came from the room and Jane's face flushed. *I'd be singing like a banshee if that was for dessert! MERCY ME! Where'd she fit all that!*

Another buzz and a new text disrupted Jane's viewing.

[Mark: I stopped by your place to bring you soup but your roommate said you were spending the weekend with your new boyfriend.]

Ouch. If he's her man, then she bailed on his ass this weekend for caliente caramel, sweetheart. Twisting her lips, her curiosity peaked. *What have you been sending, Mark? Looks like her last reply was this morning saying she had the flu and stay away. Ha! I want to catch the flu if that's what we're calling Mister Spanish Lover!*

[Mark: And apparently, that's not me.]

Oh, it's definitely not you this weekend, sweetheart. Maybe she'll cash you in next weekend? Jane snickered to herself, despite the creaking of her bed under the fucking couple annoying her. *In fact, who are these other pictures she has of... how does Mark stack up against Mr. Caliente Caramel?*

[Mark: Did you forget to break up with me or something?]

Jane ignored the text, flipping through the photo gallery. Her stomach knotted and she blinked, marveling over the dark-haired brute. Everything about him was *her type* and she cursed the girl for giving something like that up. She peeked back into the bedroom, baffled that they still had stamina, his hands gripping her hips, pushing himself deeper into her as she gasped with each thrust.

The phone started ringing and she hit ignore. *Poor guy. She's a little too busy to talk.*

Another text buzzed through and Jane cringed, watching as the couple started to peak. The man repeating over and over, *my lovely.* With a howl and deep arch, Karen's ecstasy hit, bracing against his muscular thighs as she took in his throbbing cock, both coming hard.

[Mark: Karen!! Call me ASAP!!!!!!]

Fuck this. Jane snapped a photo with Karen's phone. *Sent. Let's see if this answers your question Mark. Shouldn't be long before...*

[Mark: WHAT THE FUCK!!!!!!!!!!!!!!! FUCK YOU!!!!! YOU, CHEATING BITCH!!!!]

A smile crested Jane's face. *No one fucks in my room besides me.*

2

The Flu My Ass

Mark Wilder scowled at his cell phone, taking another swig of his beer. The broad-shouldered college Sophomore was more irritated than relaxed as his two friends narrowed their eyes at him across the table. He ran a hand through his thick black hair, stewing in anger while his leg jittered on the bar stool. His girlfriend, Karen, of almost two years, was supposed to be sick with the flu. Instead, she had other plans...

Come on. At least show me some respect. A vein pulsed in his temple, a revelation rising in his mind. *Unless, all those times she'd visited sick relatives were bullshit too... Son-of-a-bitch! She's been sleeping around on me for our entire relationship!*

"You okay, Mark? You look royally pissed." Timmy took a slow drag of his beer before leaning in. "Look, if this wasn't a good weekend for me to visit from Jersey, I could've easily grabbed a work shift. Dylan's a nice boss like that."

Mark sighed, shaking his head. "I just caught my girl cheating on me. This fucking sucks ass... dammit!"

"Ouch," Axle chimed in, arching a brow. "That sucks. You've been together for a while, right?"

Mark lowered his brow and glared back. "Thanks. I'm fully aware of that fact. And I can't help but wonder if she's been sleeping around this whole fucking time. She said she had the flu. How many other times has she faked being sick?"

"I wanna catch the flu." Axle flinched as Mark shot him an angry glare.

"Let's change topics!" Timmy flagged down a waitress. "Two buckets, one full of Bud Light and the other... you got Shiner Bock?"

"Yes, we do, though that bucket has an upcharge." She smiled, shifting so her breast bounced and called all their eyes to them. "You okay with that? I'll go grab it."

"Perfect. It's on my tab." Timmy turned back, rubbing his jawline.

Mark punched the keys on his cell phone aggressively, his face a shade of red, his emotions already past the stages of grief. He was pissed. *If she didn't want to be with me, why didn't she bother breaking up with me?* And give me the chance to screw all the girls like a normal single guy.

He sucked on his inner cheek as he hit send.

[Mark: Did you forget to break up with me or something?]

Tossing the phone upside down on the table, he drained the last of his beer, then crushed the can into the bucket. The others sat; eyes wide as they glanced at one another. Their faces told him exactly what they thought, and how he felt, *it's going to be a long night.*

"SO!" Timmy slapped the table, drawing everyone's attention to him. "Is the fraternity still doing that thing?"

"What thing?" Mark drawled.

The waitress slid two buckets onto the table and spirited away the other without a word or glance.

Mark grabbed a Shiner Bock, cracking it open. "You mean that stupid B&B thing?"

"Yeah, the hazing ritual I started!" Timmy's eyes sparkled.

"Well, it outgrew the fraternity," announced Axel, rubbing his shaved head. "Now all the local colleges compete to reserve a room. Granted, the Blue Lady has been leaving behind a trail of blue balls since you left."

"Oh shit." Timmy took a drink, looking off as if guilty for something. "It wasn't supposed to be a multi-university tradition. Shit. Oh man, she must have it out for me..."

"I don't believe in poltergeist, and why the hell would anyone from the 1800's want to fuck some college dork? Especially now that we have those horny stallions from AbraXus Tasker College mixed in?" Mark was bitter, his eye glaring at the phone. "I refuse to participate. Where did you get the ridiculous idea for this anyhow, Tim?"

"You can say, my former college at Bridgewater Trinity *inspired* me." He laughed, finishing his own beer, eyes shooting off sideways as if hiding behind a half-truth. "So, has anyone hooked up with her?"

"No, but she has been known to leave countless blue balls and dry, unenthusiastic handjobs in her wake." Axel chuckled. "Though, I don't know if I believe those stories either."

"Ghost stories," corrected Mark, rolling his eyes. "You can't convince me that some ghost woman is waiting in a small-town B&B, ready to get laid."

"Technically, only the first part is true. I was the one who declared the last part. She didn't ask for a wave of college boys to come to her rescue. In fact, why did I pick..." Timmy's eyes looked up, recalling a memory. "Oh yeah. Satch made it into a game back home; who could hook up with the most... never mind. Just know, I can't keep up with that guy, and I thought the impossible would give me an ace up the sleeve."

"Satch sounds like a man-whore." Mark chuckled. "I think it's just an excuse to go on a mini-vacation, hook up with a local girl, then call it a day."

"Last weekend, Levi swore he saw a ghost. Said in the middle of the night, someone felt him up and by morning, he was blue balling so hard he went home." Axel grabbed a Bud Light and held it a moment. "Now I know why they call them "blue" after I took him to the doctor's on Monday. It was rough stuff."

"Stop it. That annoying asshole probably got kicked in the gonads for being too bold." Timmy watched as Mark slid the phone closer, hesitating to flip the screen up. "So, Mark, did you ever go?"

"Hell no." Glaring at the phone, he took a slow sip of his beer.

"What about you, Axel?" Tim shifted. "You ever go?"

"Actually," He rubbed the back of his neck, embarrassment building on his face. "I get it next, for an entire week in fact. Like Mark said, I thought it sounded like a chance to relax, have fun, and satisfy my curiosity."

"Ha." Mark grabbed up the phone, unwilling to cave in front of his friends. "Well, I gotta piss."

Mark by passed the bathroom and slipped out the back door. Half the dive bar's patrons bar pissed on the back fence while waving to passing Amtrak trains. He relieved himself, confident no one could hear what conversation that may unfold. He dialed Karen's cell number. He zipped himself up, it rung once, and he was sent to voicemail.

Anger boiled up from his core. She knew he had caught her and now she had the gull to ignore him. *You'll have to come back home eventually, Karen!* Marching back into the bar, he punched in his next text to her.

[Mark: Karen!! Call me ASAP!!!!!!]

Hitting send, he sat there and finished his beer.

"Then who has the B&B reserved this weekend?" Tim disregarded the angry state of his friend and pressed on with the conversation.

Axel shrugged. "Some assclown from AbraXus has it. Bill? Phil? The kicker on the football team, that guy."

"Aren't they horny horses or some shit." Tim's commentary sent them into another round of chuckling.

"And what's with those colors?" At this rate, Mark was feeling depressed, but he clung to the conversation. "Pink, purple, or is that more magenta and fuchsia?"

Tim choked on his beer. "What kind of color is fuchsia?" he asked. "Is that more pink or more pur–"

A text buzzed on Mark's phone, halting the conversation as all eyes fell to the backlit screen. Mark glanced down, his face paling before shifting to maroon, veins pulsing. He lifted it up, showing the entire table the provocative image of Karen atop a caramel skinned athlete. Both faces very visible and full of pleasure. A blue light cast across them and everything about the room screamed *small-town B&B*.

You, fucking bitch. After a moment of huffing, Mark managed to get the words out. "This guy? Isn't that the kicker and your B&B with my girl on top of him?"

"Oh shit." Axel and Timmy gripped their beers.

"I can't..." Depression weighed him down and Mark covered his face in defeat.

"Look, Mark. Fuck her," declared Timmy, scooting his barstool closer. "There are way better chicks out there. Sometimes, they can walk into your life when you least expect them. Literally."

"What do you know about love?" Mark leaned on the table. "Maybe, I should convince her to stay with me? Maybe, I did something wrong?"

"No, don't you dare go down that road." Axel downed the last of his beer. "You're a good guy, Mark. She's a shitty person. It has nothing to do with you."

There was a pause, then Mark muttered, "Will I find love again?" *Depression stage initiated.*

"Nope, don't do that either." Timmy made him sit upright, pulling his hand from his puckered and pitiful expression. "Look, we never thought Dylan Johnson was the type to settle down. Then Abby walked in and changed that. You just haven't found the right girl."

"I want to see it." Mark gulped down his beer, then grabbed another from the bucket. "That stupid B&B. What was so special about it that she'd rather be there with him and not me?"

"Fine." Axel pulled out his cell phone, making several swipes on the screen. "There's my confirmation for next weekend. If it makes you feel better, you'll see she's shit and that there's nothing special about that place besides an old ghost story."

Timmy cringed, then after a minute, he smirked at the picture still glowing on the table. "If you're lucky, maybe you'll hook up with a local and get a chance to take a picture of your own. Then, send that shit to her as revenge. There's no way Karen will be happy if you break things up with her first."

Mark grabbed his phone. Karen was calling and he ignored it. A text flashed.

[Karen: I can explain!!! PICK UP!]

"Yeah. I like that idea."

[Mark: FUCK YOU. We're done.]

3

Speak to the Manager

The sun poured down, brighter than ever. Pausing from weed pulling, Jane stood and stretched her back. The quaint little garden had been laid in bricks and pavers, a collage of missing brickwork. A small bench in the shade sat before a row of hibiscus and above that, was a porch overlooking the site. A small white picket fence matched by evergreens with spurts of Japanese boxwood. For color, Mexican petunias, Wichita blue juniper, and red-tipped photinia filled in the larger sections, while spurts of perennials, in the form of a variety of lilies, occasionally filled in the gaps.

Star jasmine grew to cover the side yard mess near the building. Often, they bloomed at night, filling the air with its sweet scent. For attracting butterflies, there were rosebushes, vining plants, and an assortment of sage to maintain the appetites of hungry little caterpillars. It had taken years to get the garden to look this way, and she wasn't letting the weeds ruin them after the last gardener quit.

What a brat. To blame me as the reason to quite, when I was just trying to point his mistake when he plucked my lilies out surrounding the willow.

Glancing at her pocket watch, it was nearing check-out time. Like a staged event, the bickering disrupted the peaceful morning and brought a smile to Jane's face. By now, the boyfriend would have called. Even more wonderous, there'd be a picture of her and her caliente lover magically sent via her own text.

Jane bit her lip, getting aroused by thinking about the man's lean and gorgeous body, but her ex-lover Mark, now he's one she wanted to see sans-clothes. *That's more of my kind of fun in the sheets. What on earth would've possessed you to give him up? Greed? Lust? Is he bad in bed? I mean, you didn't even send sultry pictures to your actual boyfriend That's a problem, girlie.*

Karen marched out of the little B&B and paced the main sidewalk between the porch and gate. "Mark, I swear! It won't happen again!"

Close behind her was her lover, Phillipe. "Look, I paid for the room, but we need to go. I got practice later today."

"Shut up, Phillipe," she hissed, covering the receiver.

Phillipe threw up his hands, then marched pass her. "Look, I had a great time but unless you get in the car, you'll have to find another way home. I didn't sign up for this drama. You said you two broke it off, and everyone *knows*—you don't *fuck* with Mark Wilder. He was one of the best defensive guards before he quit."

"Dammit, Phillipe!" Her shout came through the phone, Mark's own voice blasting from the device and she doubled back. "No, baby. He's not here. I ditched him for you." Her voice softened. "I don't know who sent you that picture, but it wasn't me. We've been together six months... er... right, two years..." She cringed at her mistake. "No, I was thinking... no... Mark, please..."

There was a long pause, Phillipe stopped at the gate, watching Karen unravel. Her face beamed red, her hair a wreck from each time she'd tugged on it. Her pacing accelerated. Jane watched with amusement as her lips widened, only to be cut off from her ex-lover's words.

Karen had *fucked up*. On more than one level.

How the hell do you not know how long you've been with a man? Jane gnawed on her pipe, lighting it with a snort. *How many men has she had on the side, to muddle that number to hell? A significant difference between six months and two years.*

"It wasn't me," she pleaded, her voice trembling. "No, I mean, I'm sick, don't you remember? I have the flu." She paused, fanning herself and forcing herself to hyperventilate as if she were crying. "A-are you calling me a *liar*? How could you say that, Mark?"

Wow. She's laying it on thick. And yet not a single tear shed. Jane blew smoke from her pursed lips, making rings that circled Karen's face like a picture frame. *You're a vile one, a regular jezebel worthy of bad karma, madame. I don't even feel guilty for what I did. Sounds like I did him a huge favor!*

Karen's face twisted. "Okay, so it was me. I didn't realize you could see my tramp stamp. How the hell could... oh." She took another breath, then resumed her pacing. "Look, if you were around more then... well... I know I cancelled the last six times, but I had better things to do! I have a life too!"

She bit her lip and pulled the phone back. Mark roared, "FUCKING HALF OF ABRAXUS TASKER COLLEGE APPARENTLY!"

Jane raised her brow, crossing her arms, still grinning over the majesty of this conversation. *Oh, he's no fool, now that she's been caught. She's flailing now. Bad.*

"What? But... no you can't end our relationship!" Another fist full of hair, scowling as she hissed over the phone, "You can't break up with me! I break up–" She glared at her phone in shock. "He... he... he hung up on me!"

"Look, let's just go so I can take you home and you can clear this up." Phillipe rubbed the back of his neck.

"No." She spun on her heels, facing the B&B entrance. "I want to speak with a manager! Someone working the late shift must've taken this picture. Who else would've had a key to our room?" She marched forward, determination written on her face. "In fact, I'll get your money back."

"Oh, this ought to be good." Jane brushed the dirt off her knees and butt, then sashayed towards the porch where she could hear Karen's formal complaint. "That man will not refund that room after the mess they left in it. Hell, I don't think anyone has weaseled a refund from him. He's quick witted and the shit he knows about folks at a glance is unnerving."

"I demand a refund!" Karen had her volume on max, shifting into full attack mode. "Someone took an inappropriate photo of us! In our room! Last night!"

"Excuse me?" The manager lowered the book he'd been reading and lifted an eyebrow. "And what does that have to do with refunding you the room you slept in and made a mess in?"

Karen's face flushed once again. "I demand to know who works the night shift, who would've had access to our room."

"No one." His eyes returned to his book, his demeanor unmoved by her tantrum as he flipped to the next page. "If you hadn't noticed, we're a small family owned and operated establishment. We can't afford additional staff besides myself and the maid who cleans in the morning after guests such as yourself."

She pointed to her phone. "Someone took a photo of us."

"May I see?" He peeked over the top of the book, and she gasped.

"N-no!"

"Well, how can I verify if you're telling the truth?" He marveled, a wicked glint in his eyes.

"Haven't you heard, *the customer is always right?*" hissed Karen.

"Yes, and it's a bit dated. As I recall, that term coined during the wild west days when customers were more honest and loyal." Clearing his throat, he said, "Produce proof or I can't dispute your claim."

"I'm not showing you a picture of... of..." Her face turned a deeper shade of red.

"Who else stayed in that room besides you? Did you ask them if they took the picture?" Another arching eyebrow silenced Karen, deflating some of her ego.

Jane puffed on her pipe of cherry tobacco, watching as Karen marched out and towards Phillipe. She snickered. The gir was a force to be reckoned with when mad. Though, her circumstance was of her own creation. Taking a puff of the pipe, she watched as the next round of shouting began. Karen was out for blood, and it didn't matter who was injured in the process.

"Did you do this?" She held up her phone to her Spanish lover. "Did you take this?"

"Take what?" Phillipe unlatched the gate, baffled. "Let's go already. Now, you're embarrassing me, and I can't be late for practice."

"Did you take this picture of us fucking, then sent it to Mark?" she declared.

"No. How could I when I was stuck under you, while you cowgirl styled my dick with your pussy." He laughed, shaking his head. "Come on. Let's go."

She was rendered speechless as she followed Phillipe out to the main sidewalk, then descended the path. Jane stood, watching as they went.

Karen paused in her steps, taking a double look.

Again, her face flushed, and she stormed to the fence. Inhaling deep, she shouted with all her might. "YOU! YOU THERE IN BLUE!"

Phillipe looked to where she shouted, confused. "Who in the hell are you screaming at?"

"The gardener," she hissed. But when she turned back, Jane had disappeared. "The... woman. In blue."

"Real funny." He continued walking, shaking his head. "It's just a ghost story."

"Are you calling me a liar?" she asked as she chased after him. "This is the third *fucking* time I've been accused of lying today! This is bullshit!"

Jane took a few more puffs of her pipe. She had sat on the garden bench, fully aware the hedgerow and old willow blocked her from of view. They were long gone, the birds continued to sing and the butterflies fluttered above the garden.

The manager appeared on the front porch and yawned, then he choked on her pipe smoke. "Dammit, Jane. That can't be good for people." It was a statement more than a threat. "Not like anyone can stop you."

Jane smiled to herself, dumping the last of her pipe tobacco. "Fine, you win. I'll cut it out for the rest of the day. You earned enough of my respect after the way you handled that unruly woman."

"Man, she *was* a bitch." He scratched his jaw, then lowered his gaze to the garden. "Man, you'd think I hired a professional gardener. I suppose I should say thank you."

"You're welcome." She stood, walking around the willow tree, admiring her handiwork. "But you still need to hire a gardener. I'm getting too old for this."

"Yeah, I'll make a couple calls. I wonder if old man Ted still runs his landscaping business."

"Oh man, is that where he ended up doing? Landscaping." She grinned and squatted to pluck a weed from between the pavers. "And to think he nearly crashed his car through this very garden as a kid. Life spins us in funny ways."

Looking up, the manager had disappeared inside, making Jane's chest ached. She hated the way it snuck up on her, that drowning sensation of being alone and depressed. Ever since her husband left this world, she couldn't bear to see everything that stood for him and their relationship go to ruin. This was the home they had shared before he passed. She couldn't let it rot away so easily, even if she no longer owned it.

Besides, I'm too ornery to die just yet...

4

The Gardener

Mark stood before the B&B with mixed emotions. Much to his disappointment, there wasn't much to the place. He could confirm they didn't hook up in a romantic setting. Old vegetation covered the building, while paint peeled off the two-story building that should've fallen down decades ago. Adjusting the duffel bag strap on his shoulder, he pushed through the tiny gate.

Halfway down the front walkway, he paused, covering his face. *What the hell am I doing here? Why the fuck would I stay in a room where my ex-girlfriend cheated on me?*

Inhaling deep, he held it. Then buried his turbulent emotions rolling in his chest deep once more. Looking back to the building, he realized he hadn't seen any signage. Circling back to the gate, he checked it and came up blank. Craning his neck , he spotted someone in the garden. Curious to know if he had found the right place or some old man's house, he cleared his throat, announcing himself.

The girl bent over, pulling weeds from the base of an old willow tree, didn't flinch. His eyes wondered across her body, everything about her was *his type*. The baby blue jean cut offs with brass rivets fit her ass tightly, leaving little to the imagination for what lay in between. Her skin peeked out of the top before escaping into her light blue crop top.

At this angle, he had a glance her soft blue lacy bra, and his breath hitched. *Holy shit, she's gorgeous.*

She shuffled over and continued pulling weeds surrounding a batch of lilies. Her hands were in leather gloves, her arms muscular, and sweat rolled down the side of her cheek. Far as he could tell, she had been at this all morning. A hat obscured the top half of her face, nothing but high cheekbone and pale pink lips making him aroused.

What am I doing? Just standing here like a creepy stalker with a hardon? Say something!

"Excuse me." His eyes darted away, sliding his duffle bag to block the bulge inside his jeans. "Is this the Story Bed & Breakfast?"

Again, she kept working and Mark wondered if he had mumbled his words. Squatting down, he made himself semi-eyelevel with her, tapping her arm to make her aware of his presence.

She froze. Slowly, she turned to face where his fingers met her arm, before tracing the appendage until their eyes met. Pimples rolled across her tan skin, and he held his breath like he had disturbed the surface of a glassy lake.

Wide eyed, her blue eyes seemed to glow in the light. "Are you..." She squinted, reading his face. "Are you touching me?"

"Sorry, I didn't mean to startle you." He blinked, unsure of how to gauge her reaction. "Wait, shit, are you deaf?"

"What? No!" She laughed, shaking her head. "I'm not. Not many people show up here wanting to chat with the gardener, is all. They kind of don't notice me most of the time, if not, *all* the time. I'm sorry, what are you asking me?"

"Well, you were the first person I saw." She motioned for him to stand, and he did so, hugging the duffle bag to his front as his eyes dipped to her flushed cleavage. "Is this, uh, is this the Story B&B?"

"Yes, it is. It's been here for as long as the town, in fact." They walked side-by-side, then stopped when they reached the main entrance. "The manager should be in there, reading his book. I don't think they have any other guests here besides an old couple in town visiting for a family reunion."

Mark took in the admiration on her face. "You love this place. Why?"

Her face flushed and she locked eyes with him. "Well, my... well, it was in the family name for some time."

Shit! She was an owner! And I'm eating her alive like eye candy!

Mark's face turned red. "I'm sorry! I'm Mark, Mark Wilder and you are?"

"Jane..." He held out a hand and she smirked, pulling her own from the gardening gloves and gripped it tight. "Just Jane."

"Little old fashioned."

She paled. "What's old fashioned?"

"Your name, Jane. I like it." Mark looked to the entrance, then back at Jane. "Do you stay here or live in the area?"

"Yeah... you can say I live here at the B&B." Her eyes scanned him from head to toe, lingering on his lips once more. "Are you checking in or applying for the gardening job?"

He blinked. "Checking in. And no offense, it seems like you have this under control? Or are you retiring?"

"Retiring..." She tilted her head, arching her eyebrows. "I'm just stepping in to maintain the B&B's most important feature. I can't have the place full of weeds and falling apart."

Mark gave her another scan, licking his lips and running his hand through his hair. "I don't normally do this, but..." *What the hell did I have to lose?* "Would you like to join me upstairs in the shower?"

Jane opened her mouth and paused.

Mark held his breath, unsure if he'd been too bold or offended her.

He watched as she covered her mouth, gazing at her unfinished work. Again, his eyes flowed over to her sharp jawline, her slender neck, and the way her collarbone returned his stare back to her freckled chest. A hint of the lacy blue bra dared to peek out of her crop top. At last, she swiveled her face back to him, her expression obscured by her hand as she looked him up and down.

Unable to take the growing embarrassment, Mark turned and started up the steps. "I'm sorry, forget it. That was–"

"Which room?" Her voice made him stop, and he twisted to face her, but all he could see was her back. "I'm long overdue for some fun of that kind."

Mark shook his head, taking a moment to absorb her answer. "Uh, my friend booked the... um, the..." He dug into his pockets, pulling out a folded paper and unraveled it. "Blue room?"

"Really?" At last, she shot a glance over her shoulder, her eyes glowing bright in the sunlight. "I'll be up in a moment, just gotta put away some things."

"R-right!" He couldn't contain the smile on his face. "Let me check in and... see you upstairs, Jane."

He rushed through the front door and the manager put his book down. "Checking in? Mister Axel... oh. No. Mark Wilder. Aren't you a lucky man today?"

"Yes, sir, that's me." Mark pulled his wallet out, but the manager pulled a key fob and key from the hook and slid it to him. "Upstairs on the left. The blue door. It's all been paid for."

"Um, don't you need my ID or something." The manager had returned to his book, waving Mark on as he lost himself to the novel. "I guess not..."

Mark snatched the key, then raced upstairs. On the second landing, he spotted the room with the plaque immediately, and as promised, bearing a blue door. Reaching for the knob, it creaked open and he paused, confused. *Did the maid forget to lock it or is it a faulty knob?* Pushing into the room, he closed the door, pushing it tight and checking the lock.

"It's not broken." Jane's voice jolted him, and there she stood in the room, her hat and gloves gone. "I just beat you here, is all."

"I see that." Mark flipped the lock, biting his bottom lip in anticipation. "Just going to dump the duffle at the foot of the bed and..."

He let it slide off his shoulder, rolling the stiff muscle as he turned to face her. The silence between them lingered, awkward and enthralling. Her brown hair clung to her sweat-soaked face, and he reached out to brush it from her brow. She cupped his hand, the gauging look meeting his eyes as if she somehow knew him, recognized him from somewhere.

Mark leaned in, his lips hovering so close to hers the heat of them teased of what could happen next. *Am I being too bold? Is she afraid... of this sudden desire to just be lustful for a moment in my life?*

Jane's fingers balled his shirt in them, and she yanked him forward, their lips connecting. She deepened the kiss and what hesitation that haunted him dissolved. He moaned into her mouth, enjoying the way their tongues tangled with one another. Her body was hot against his as he pulled her into him. She seemed hungry to have his passion, never slowing the voracity of her kissing as he weaseled his hand under the back of her crop top.

With a fluid motion, he had unlatched the back of her bra, and she broke the kiss with a laugh.

"You're good." She buried her face into his chest. "I have to admit, it's been a while."

"That's okay." He snorted. "To be honest, I'm on the rebound after catching my ex cheating on me."

Her fingers snaked down his chest, rolling over his abdomen and began unbuckling his pants. "Then let me help you forget all about her." She had pulled away from him some, now unbuckling her own jeans as if to make the playing field fair. "I have to confess; this isn't something I normally do. Hooking up for the fun of it."

"Really? And here I thought you were only saying yes to the shower," he teased, pulling his shirt off in a rush. "To be honest, I didn't think you'd say yes." All he desired was to feel her, touching his skin, the thought made him harder with each passing moment.

"I didn't think I'd say yes either." She laughed, removing her top and bra, letting them fall to the floor. "You okay with a hot shower?" Her hips swung left and right, her jean shorts rolling off her hips.

Blue lacy thongs... that's not proper gardening undergarments. Mark smirked. *But I'm not complaining!*

5

Hot Shower

He may look like my husband, but that body and cock is on a whole new level.

Jane's heart raced as she led Mark to the bathroom, jeans left on the threshold and her thongs sliding past her knees. He rushed to the doorway, struggling to kick off his own jeans as they tangled at his feet. They both laughed, the excitement and lust building between them took them into an unexpected ride.

She reached in, turning on the shower. Steam started to fill the span, goosebumps waving over her skin.

He doesn't have to know how long it's been since you let someone touch you. She swallowed back the nervous tension building at her core as he freed his last foot. *He doesn't know the last man you were intimate with was your belated husband.* Mark locked eyes with her, and he smiled, making her heart flutter. *They look so much alike, but...*

Her breath caught as he closed the gap between them. Lips pressing against hers and again she deepened it. She wanted to feel the heat of his body against hers, anywhere and everywhere all at once. The loneliness that had haunted her, kept her in such a restless state, slowly started to fade to the throes of passion.

They stumbled into the walk-in shower, the hot water pelting them. Her back pressed against the cold tiles and she pulled his body against hers.

His erection slid between her thighs, making her loins throb with want. Rivulets of hot water flowed down their bodies, the rush of it streaming down his back, to where her hands clung to him. *I want to feel alive again.* She rubbed her tongue against his, diving into his mouth and he throbbed between her thighs once more. His hands belonged to someone used to hard labor, the callouses adding to the visceral sensation travelling down the sides of her torso before squeezing her ass cheeks. Another throb of his cock, his hips tilting slowly to rub it against her pussy, making her wet.

Their kiss broke and they stared at one another, marveling over their instant connection. She couldn't slow her beating heart or the way her breath quickened with excitement. He began kissing her neck, and she leaned all her weight against the wall, arching and stretching so he could have full access to her body. Mark's hands slid across her hips, up her abdomen until they groped a breast in each palm.

She moaned, this time tilting her hip to slide her pussy across the top of his dick. He moaned into her neck, sucking and licking, building a hickie that she'd gladly wear. *To be touched like this... with no barriers, no restrictions, and...*

Her hands flowed across the muscular torso, diving between them where she could rub and grip his cock. Again, he moaned and throbbed against her. *I've never wanted sex with someone so desperately. This might be my only chance.*

She stroked him with one hand, and he hardened in her palm. Biting her lip, she dove her other hand inside her pussy.

Her fingers slick, she guided his erection between into her pussy. Both of them moaned as he pressed deep inside her.

Dropping a hand from a breast, it gripped her thigh and lifted it to his hip. The angle made her gasp as he thrusted, slow and steady, in and out. He abandoned his play at her neck, eyes locked on her face. She kept one hand between where they connected, enjoying how the base of his cock slid between her fingers, the shaft long and hard, slippery from her pussy.

As he gathered speed, she arched further, her other hand braced on his shoulder and he tightened his grip on her thigh.

"Don't stop," she breathed. "I don't have ovaries... please, don't stop."

Another throb escaped his dick and she moaned. "Did you just give me the greenlight to cum inside you?" He pushed deeper inside her and froze, taking in her face. "Are you sure? No chance of... you know..." His eyes dropped to her belly.

She laughed. "I said don't stop, Mark." She grinded against him, tightening around the hard cock inside her, and he grunted. "I need ovaries for that to happen."

He smirked. "But I wanted this to last a little longer. You feel so good, and... and..."

She abandoned her grip on his cock, pulling him to her so she could whisper into his ear. "Don't stop. I'm almost there, please..."

He rocked in and out, and she arched again, her head pressing hard against the tiled wall. The hot water did nothing to cool the heat building between them as their arousal began to peak. He kissed her neck, leaving a trail across her collarbone and she shuddered. Lips wrapped around a nipple, hot as his teeth pinched it and she tightened. Mark thrusted faster, fucking her harder as he latched onto her breast, aggressive and hungry.

"Yes... a little... more..." Her eyes shut tight, her body buzzing with the rising orgasm.

Adjusting his grip on her thigh, he lifted it higher and she felt them connect deeper. Another thrust against her, hard and eager, and her orgasm peaked. A scream of pleasure escaped her lips. Fingernails biting into his skin sent him moaning as her pussy tightened in waves on his rock-hard cock. He slowed, moaning into her breasts as he too came. At last, he pressed his pelvis hard against her, throbbing inside her as they rode out their orgasms as one.

Releasing her nipple, he panted and leaned on the shower wall. "Holy shit."

"You're good." Her whole body vibrated, a mixture of wanting and ecstasy. "Or I just went too long without."

He laughed, shaking his head. "Honestly, that's the best I've had... and I don't know if it's the fact we just hooked up out of left field."

Jane laughed, pressing a short and fleeting kiss him to his lips. "I wouldn't mind doing that again."

Mark arched a brow. "Really?"

He slid himself out, enjoying the hourglass figure against the hodge-podge of tiles in all shades of blue. A shudder shook her, the lack of his body heat making her skin pimple and nipples erect. Jane watched how his eyes took her body in and they followed her hands. She fondled her breasts before sliding down her torso and dove between her thighs. Diving her fingers between her folds she pulled his cum over her clit. The sensation riveting as she started to pleasure herself.

"That's no fair." He watched, his cock losing its hardness. "I have a good five minutes before I get hard again."

"Oh?" She grinned, gripping her breast with the other hand as she dipped her fingers once more between her swollen pussy. "Only five minutes?"

He ran a hand through his hair and shrugged. "I timed it."

Rolling her eyes, she focused on keeping the buzz of her orgasm rolling. Wanting to play with herself more, she pulled her cum-covered fingers back to her clit, circling the swollen jewel. With his eyes on her, she moaned enjoying the provocativeness of what she allowed herself to do in his presence. Everything about this was more erotic than she had ever been willing to do or attempt to do in her past. She began rocking her hips, lingering on the way he had felt inside her, the way his body against hers had felt. Her eyes closed and her body tensed. She was nearing a second orgasm, and she dipped her finger in and out, frustrated that she couldn't bring back the pleasure he had bestowed her.

"Let me help with that." His voice gruffed into her ear, breath hot against her neck.

Again, the string of kisses at her neck made her shiver with anticipation. Lips burnt a trail down her body, only pausing to tease a nipple before licking and sucking down her stomach. She abandoned her play, wanting to only feel him and the way he touched her. He kept going, lower than any man had been on her until her breath caught. Shouldering one of her legs, the heat of his mouth wrapped around her clit and she shrieked, body folding onto him.

How long I've waited just to feel another person's touch, but this isn't what I had in mind! She bit her lip, snuffing the thoughts out so she could enjoy every intimate moment.

One strong arm road back up her body, unfolding her and placing her flat against the tiles once more. Her eyes wide, fingers tangling in his hair, her mouth opened but was at a loss for words. Like he'd done to her nipple, the tip of his tongue circled her clit and she gasped. It was electrifying, shooting through her body, and building on her orgasm in a way she didn't know possible. She fought with herself, unsure to pull him away or hold him into her.

Do I dare say I feel alive again? What is it about this man that makes him different from all the others who have come here in search of a night with the Blue Lady?

He moaned into her pussy and she rocked into him. She didn't want him to stop. He kissed her there as deeply as he had done with her lips and her heart pounded with excitement. Shifting, she opened her thighs a little wider, wanting more. He responded to the motion, breaking his suckling from her clit made her squeak. Hot and silky, he ran his tongue across her throbbing opening, teasing that he may dip his tongue inside. She inhaled deep and swift, holding it there as her knees began to shake.

What on earth did he just do to my body! Can I even stay standing at this rate?

6

Hungry Lover

Mark stole a glance at Jane's face and smirked.

She's never had someone go down on her!

The idea he would be the first excited him, though he hated the refractory period, even if he had been blessed with a five-minute wait unlike some of his colleagues. Still, seeing her please herself with his cum had made him hot and bothered. He wanted to keep playing with her, pleasuring her for his own lustful desires. Teasing the opening of her pussy, dripping wet with his playful suckling, her legs shook.

Good girl... opening those legs for Daddy.

He pushed his tongue between the folds, licking inside her pussy like a hot apple pie. She moaned, rocking her hips in a way that let him taste her further, deeper. Her fingers gripped his hair and she began losing herself to the sensation of his hungry eating. The moaning and gasps grew, her hips rocking faster against his face. Tensing as the roughness of his five o'clock shadow prickled into her sensitive flesh. Holding onto her leg against his shoulder, he sucked and slurped, moaning into her pussy. Again, her legs shook.

He reached down, rubbing his cock. *Just a little longer... I'm slowly getting hard again.*

Rolling his tongue up, he returned to her clit. Wrapping his lips on her hard-swollen bean and sucked long and hard. She folded over him, his arm gone and unable to keep her stretched against the wall. His cock throbbed in his palm. He didn't want her to come, not until he could bend her over and be back inside her to enjoying the tight pulsing of how hard she came like before. He wanted that one more time. He wanted to feel her orgasm on his dick.

This might be the only time I hook up with her.

He flicked his tongue on the jewel and she shrieked, legs wobbling to the point she slid down on the wall. Every muscle in her body locked and shook. He had her teetering and he slowed his playful eating to allow her to waver off the edge. That he would save for her he pounded her to his delight.

I'm going to savor everything I can from this moment. I want to enjoy every second of this as long as she's willing to keep going. As long as she can keep up with me...

She braced herself on the shower walls, releasing his hair. The water pouring over them turned cold as her searching hand knocked into the knob. The chilling streams added to the visceral sensations rattling them. He throbbed in his palm.

That's it, just a little harder...

He abandoned her clit and began kissing up her body to the other breast and sampled the nipple, hard against the tip of his tongue. His hand slid between her thighs and he thrust two fingers inside. She leaned into him, unable to fold over with his body against hers. They both shivered under the icy water, neither of them willing to break away from the heat of their passion to right the mistake. He thrust in and out of her, enjoying how she tightened on his fingers. With his other hand, he stroked himself, his erection almost to its peak once more. Catching her nipple in his teeth, her pussy tightened. The sensation of it finally making him rock hard. At last, he released her breast.

"Turn around," he huffed, goosebumps making him shudder.

She tilted her head, confused. "Why?"

Mark searched her eyes a moment before smirking. "Forgive me for asking but..." He licked his lips before leaning into her ear. "Is it wrong to assume you've only done missionary style?"

Her hands balled against his chest and her body stiffened in defense at the comment. She didn't say a word. Sensing her rising anger and embarrassment, he began suckling on her ear. A shiver shook her. Sliding his fingers out of her, he gripped her hips and spun her into position, rubbing his hard cock between her thighs. Her body heated under him in response, excited at the thought he was ready again. She reached down and he gripped her wrists.

"It's my turn to play with you," he demanded.

Holding her wrist above her head, he held them tight against the tiles. Watching between them, he rubbed the tip of his cock against her hot pussy. Shuffling, she spread her legs a little wider and tilting her hip. He pressed hard and slipped inside. Again, she tightened around him, inhaling swift as he pressed his length all the way inside. At first, he rocked in and out, slow and agonizing. Her legs trembled, body still riding on the pleasure of their foreplay. With each thrust, his cock grew harder and slicker.

Look at you, being naughty and trying something new.

Jane panted, pinned between his body and the tiles. As he gained momentum, she moaned, pushing her ass against him to allow him to full access. His body buzzed, his own orgasm already threatening to end his fun earlier than expected for his second time. Releasing her wrists, his hands rode down her arms and to the front of her torso. He groped a breast in one hand while the other hand continued to snake downward. Like she had done before, he mimicked her motion feeling where his cock slid in and out of her. He moaned as she tensed around his throbbing dick.

Shit, I'm going to come too fast.

Changing tactics, he pulled her hips away from the wall. The cold water blasting over him, knocking back the rising orgasm. She moaned at the new angle, rocking herself on his dick. His hands retreated to her hips and he watched his length pull out of her before slowly entering her. Each time he swore her body gushed and rattled with delight, gasps coming from her. At last she looked over her shoulder with a pitiful expression.

"Please..." she begged.

He locked eyes with her, watching the pleasure on her face as he pushed slow and teasingly back inside her wanton heat. "Please?"

"Faster." She braced herself on the wall. "I want you to go faster."

His cock throbbed inside her and she tightened in response. "Faster or harder?"

Her brow knitted. "I don't know what either of those mean."

A laugh escaped him. "You're amazing."

"Don't laugh." Her face flushed. "I just, I didn't think I'd like this so much and you're not fucking me fast enough."

"Hard enough," he corrected with a smirk. "Faster means you want me to come sooner. Harder means you want me to thrust more aggressively."

Puffing out her cheeks, she looked back to the wall. "Fuck me harder."

"Then stand up straighter, I don't need you breaking your nose against the tiles." Mark chuckled, liking their exchange. "We can't do it here at this angle."

"I'll be fine, fuck me hard just like this," she inhaled deep, holding it to wait for the onslaught of whatever she thought she enacted.

"Jane, if you like this angle, then we should move to the bed." He shut off the water and pulled away from her to grab a towel.

I can use this to back off my orgasm some and gain back some lost ground.

"Don't leave. I wasn't done." She stood in alarm. "I don't understand how the bed will help. I'm enjoying it just fine in the shower."

His eyebrows lifted high at the tantrum she started to throw. "Glad you approve, but..." He bit his lip a moment as his eyes trailed down to her knees. "But I don't think your knees will be able to hold you up much longer. You got pretty wobbly there."

Looking to her legs, she looked betrayed. "Well, if you insist and promise to go... harder."

Mark snorted. "The whole B&B might hear us, but how can I say no."

Jane paled. "Can they hear us?" She rushed pass him, covering her face. "Oh... is it like that one couple? Where... Aunt May called the manager? I don't think I can live with myself."

Mark spun her, shoving her forward until she stumbled into the bed. "Let them hear us."

"M-mark!" Before she could stand up straight, his cock slid inside her. "Ooh!"

Her fists balled the blanket in them, and his fingers dug tight into her hips. He wasted no time, her breasts swaying as her grinded hard and fast against her. The bed squeaked as they rocked against it. Her ass slapped against his thighs, her body growing hot under his reckless thrusting. She could only gasp, growing tighter with each inhale. Moaning, he was starting to peak unable to resist how her heat wrapped around his rock-hard cock. A screech escaped her, a gush of hot fluid rushing between them.

Oh, we came hard... I guess it's my turn to make a mess.

He held onto her, trying his best to not lose his momentum. At last, he couldn't hold back as he too peaked. Pressing hard against her, he groaned as he came. Her back arched and she grinded into him, fingers gliding to touch where they connected. A shiver rattled through his spine.

Something about how she wants to feel where I slide inside her just makes this so much sweeter.

Releasing her hips, he glided under her, groping her breasts, and pulling her to stand and lean into him. She touched and played with herself, all while he still lingered inside her pussy. He kissed her neck and shoulders, massaging her breasts. The cherry tobacco smell wafted from her hair. He inhaled deep, holding the scent as she rocked her hips riding out her orgasm. As her breath caught and began to whimper, he bit her shoulder and pinched her nipples. Her pussy grew tight, and he had found her preference: *Jane liked it rough.*

Did she just come again? How many times was that for her?

"Feel better?" He cooed as the tension in her body melted away.

"I haven't felt anything in a while..." Swallowing, she caught her breath. "Now what?"

Hugging onto her, he inhaled the tangy scent once more. "How about you spend the whole weekend here in this room with me? No obligations, just you and me enjoying each other like this until my time's up." Nuzzling her neck, he kissed it.

"I can't say I'm not curious to see what else you can do with this." Her finger rubbed where they were still connected, his hardness fading.

He laughed, pulling away, then fell on his back atop the bed. "Forgive me, Jane. I think I need a nap." Managing to grab her wrist, he tugged her onto the bed beside him. "How about we rest up and start this again when we wake up?"

His eyelids felt heavy, drained , worse than what he normally felt after two sessions.

Was it the drive that drained me? Maybe all the stress with Karen and being able to just, let it all go just now.

He could feel her fingers pacing to and fro along his forearm, the muscles twitching and a smile coming to his face.

I don't think I've ever been with a girl who prefers it rough. Fuck, Karen. I think I'm in love with Jane.

7

Something for Later

Mark had fallen asleep fast and she covered him up before bolting through the door. She felt like a runaway bride, the way she hesitated at the top of the stairs to steal one last look at the closed door. Shaking herself from the longing and haunting sensations of his hot hands all over her body, she let herself break away. Once more, Jane puffed her cheeks out and rushed down the steps. For a moment, she thought the manager saw her rush out the front door. The way he had stiffened and peeked over the book, looking where she had just flown down the steps as if he heard the tapping of her feet.

There's no way he saw me too! What the hell is happening to me? Who is this Mark Wilder, really?

Stumbling to a stop on the porch, she sidled to her spot on the top step and sat. Eyes wide with racing thoughts, she searched her pockets for the pipe and tobacco tin. It didn't take her long to pack the pipe and strike a match on the wood post to bring the smoking behemoth to life. A long pull brought her nerves to a calm, her panic slowing to a dull roar as she held it in for a minute and released it.

Did that really happen?

The smoke curled from her lips like a bad omen and her blue eyes glowed. Looking at the willow tree, she could see where she stopped pulling the weeds and her chest ached. For the last few weeks, she had just kept the garden going, until someone more skilled and permanent could be hired. Sure, she had made a few people do double-takes during the day as of late, but none of it had been ill-intended. Not like you'd expect from a poltergeist.

"I didn't even know he was talking to me." Mumbling to herself, she didn't bother to pull the pipe from her lips. "No one talks to the gardener, and no one openly approaches apparitions of the Blue Lady either."

Rubbing her forehead, she thought back to last weekend. Upstairs was the man Karen had abandoned and somehow landed himself in her room and bed. Worse, how could she say no to...

"Son of a bitch." She gnawed on the pipe as her frustration rose. "What the hell was I thinking following that kid upstairs. But shit, who could say no? I've been... the last time I could... I mean, it was my husband and I, dating back... no one could say no to an offer like that. It seemed like a miracle and..."

Goosebumps rolled over her skin. After a few more puffs of her pipe, she pulled one more item from her pocket: *Mark's cell phone.* A mischievous grin crossed her face. Part of her was disappointed as she searched the most private areas of his phone. Unlike his beloved Karen's gallery, he had no dick pics and apparently, she never bothered to share any pussy shots with him, not even a decent nipple or cleavage shot.

Raw deal. The heat rose in her face over this idea. *What a nasty whore. Lock in that man and not provide him with eye candy like her boy toys. She did him dirty. Someone needs to make it up to that man. Two years of dry spell...*

Pursing her lips to hold the pipe, she let it hover over own cleavage. Her upper arms squeezed her girls together, pushing them up and her blue lacy bra slid out of the low-cut crop top. A couple of clicks and she took a look around. The B&B was quiet and the town all around lifeless for a Saturday evening. Goaded by the thought she could fill the gap Karen left in Mark's gallery, she sashayed to the side yard where the shade of large bushes and unkempt lilies might offer great photo mates.

If she won't give it to him, I will!

Right on cue, a text buzzed through, dumping Jane from camera mode.

"Speak of the devil."

[Karen: Mark, let's meet up. I want to talk. Please, let me make this up to you.]

Jane pulled the pipe from her lips. Smoke billowing out and slamming against the screen. Dumping her pipe out, she smirked as her fingers tapped away with authority.

[Mark: The Blue Lady Room. Midnight.]

She watched as the text status shifted from delivered to read. Karen began to type more, but Jane was faster, blocking the number. She chuckled, satisfied with the plan she had cooked up. Her eyes took in the overgrown cubby of foliage all around.

"If I can't see out, no one should be able to see in." Flipping back to the camera, she thought back to Karen's naughty pictures. "Fuck her. I can do better. Someone's about to have the rarest footage of the B&B's very own Jane Story in the nude."

With a snap of her fingers, her clothes shifted into a vintage white petticoat and corset. She shook her hair out of the bun and snapped a downward shot, catching her smirk and cleavage in the sultry shot. After a few clicks, she pulled the phone to her to evaluate her handiwork. Her heart fluttered, the idea of what she would be leaving behind for him thrilling and arousing. Inhaling deep, she reached back and began unlacing her corset.

Something tells me he's going to really appreciate these.

An ache swelled in her chest and she swallowed it down. Flicking her fingers, the phone floated in the air, hovering around snapping shots. On occasion she would look to the phone, giving him a look, one she knew he'd understand the weight of after what they had done moments before. Jane paced herself, shedding the corset and the petticoat. The phone captured her at all different angles until she found herself in the nude among the fading sunlight.

Now, what do I take pictures of?

Blinking, she pondered and shook her head.

Am I really going that far?

Staring at the phone, a flash of his smile and hungry eyes on her body made her body buzz with want.

Yeah, I'm fucking going all in.

She found herself sitting on the grass, goosebumps rolling across her skin like ripples on a lake. Gathering her courage, she aimed to relax, focus on close and erotic shots of her body. Peaks of hard nipples and self-groping, her own hand sliding down her torso, and her sucking on her own fingers. The thought he would see these, see her so raw and vulnerable, and would even pleasure himself looking at them made her arousal grow. Her pussy throbbed with want and she caved to the final round of photos she aimed to leave him.

He just makes me want to touch myself more...

Her thighs parted and she began to roll her finger over her swollen jewel. The other hand groped her breast, fingers pinching her nipple in an attempt to mimic how he had groped them. Pictures snapped, catching every play and the moment her finger dove between her pink folds. A moan escaped her, biting her lip to muffle his name. Her entire body shook with the rising orgasm, the lingering thoughts, and thrills of how his cock thrusted in and out.

Fuck, I want him back inside me one more time...

Body arching, she inhaled sharp as the stimulation peaked. The arousal and ecstasy slamming into her. More clicks of the camera caught as her juices gushed from her, fingers pulling out of the way to show him all that she offered, all that he had taken enjoyment of and how much she wanted him all over again. Panting from the orgasm, she flipped through the phone. Some photos she deleted, *we can't have blurred or half-assed shots like she had.* She intentionally cherry-picked the ones she wanted, the stolen glances, the sultry moment of her body reacting to thoughts of him. Those where she hoped she could get a literal rise out of him and his cock.

"Dammit." Her smile faltered and she frowned. "How in the hell can I explain to him that I'm nothing more than a ghost?"

Closing her eyes, she anguished over the idea. Thoughts mangled; honesty obscured by passion. The leaves rustled and she snapped her eyes open, relieved to see it was nothing more than the breeze.

Whatever reaction I had with him is fading, I didn't feel the breeze in the same level. In fact, after he touched me, I could feel again. The heat of the sun, the tickle of s strand of hair on my face, and the sliding of sweat on my skin. Sure, I can physically manipulate things and sweat under the sun, but there's another layer I've been missing since I died all those centuries ago.

The phone buzzed again, and she pulled it up.

[Timmy: Hey, how's it going?]

Twisting her lips, she sat up and snapped once more. Like that, she was back to her crop top now paired with cutoff shorts. Prying into his phone, she found a picture of the friend and furrowed her brow. Zooming in she blinked, and rage filled her.

Without further ado, she called this Timmy to have a word with him and the chaos he had thrown in her direction.

"Hey, Mark!" Timmy answered immediately. "How's it going?"

"You!" Jane fussed over the phone. "You're that pukwudgie that started this mess!"

Silence fell over the phone.

"You better not hang up or I will find a way to come haunt your ass over this bullshit!" She stood and began pacing, throwing an arm out. "You came here, found me, and after that I've been dealing with a flood of college boys invoking my name for sex like I'm some loose floozy handing out sex in handbaskets! Are you kidding me? Do I look like I'm running a paranormal whorehouse, you little creep!"

"I... I can explain..."

"Then explain it to me." She crossed her arms, fuming.

"It's about Mark." He hesitated.

"Yes?" her heart fluttered, the conversation steering in a different way then she had expected. "What about Mark?" *Was this never about me?*

"You see, I don't think he knows." Clearing his throat, he lowered his voice. "He keeps hooking up with all these girls, but he's draining them. Not on purpose, I don't think he knows he's doing it and well, they don't last long in bed with him and... I just thought. If I found someone for him... like you?"

Jane's brow folded and covered her mouth as she tried to grasp what he was trying to say. *Fucking pukwudgies, always beating around the bush and meddling. Anything to cause a bit of chaos...*

"I heard about you haunting the inn. It's not often an entity stays in an active place that long, so I thought if I could just entice him to go there, that maybe if you two meet and well..."

"Well what?" She shook her head, still grasping for what Timmy was implying. "Exactly what does Mark not know about himself that your mischief causing kind would take stock in?"

"Ask him about his dad." The comment was blunt. "You're from the Victorian days, you remember the superstitions about the co-walker? Wraith doppelgangers?"

Jane swallowed, her mind reaching for a time she had let go of ages ago. "The shadow guardians who fulfill dying wishes. The male banshee stories. When you see your doppelganger, death is coming for you. That story?"

"I think he's part wraith." Jane inhaled as Timmy pitched his suspicions. "Wait, if you have his phone, what happened? Is he okay?"

"What makes you an expert on spirits and the undead?" she demanded, blood rushing.

"I majored in Celestial and Spirit Anatomy."

"Gross," Jane muttered.

"Bear with me... and a PhD in Undead and Necromancy."

"I thought you were a casino bellhop?" she countered, questioning the trickster creature on the phone.

"Yeah, because a Jersey Devil works there."

She rubbed her forehead. "Of course, and you needed an in to get close and cause mischief."

"Maybe," he cooed. "My magic knows no boundaries."

"Yeah, I've noticed." Swallowing, she double backed to the initial fact. "He doesn't know?"

"Pretty sure of it." There was a long pause, a huff, then he added, "He doesn't know your dead. That you're a ghost."

"I noticed."

"So, what makes him different? Can he touch you? Turn you on?"

Jane's face flushed. "You, little creep."

With that she hung up the phone, coming out of the bushes to watch Mark leave the inn. She waited until he crossed the street and headed for the convenience store. Returning to her spot on the steps, she sat there feeling sick to her stomach. Lifting her pipe, she abandoned it. Shaking her head, she marched back to the bushes, looking through the gallery of photos wondering if she should just wipe them out.

Shit, not even smoking will bring my nerves to a calm. How could he not know?

8

Cherry Tobacco

Mark sat up in bed, shuddering awake from his slumber. The sunlight had started to change hues outside, and he reached over to find Jane gone. His chest ached seeing her clothes had disappeared from the floor as well. Holding his head, he fell straight back and groaned. It had been amazing, but for the first time he had run out of energy first. Usually the girl bailed, or practically suffered a narcolepsy level nap session by the time he could get off twice.

Dammit, what a bad time for a nap. And to think, to hook up with a girl so willing to try new shit and inexperienced and enjoying herself. Wonder if she'll come back...

Cherry tobacco lingered in his nostrils, he could still smell her on him and in the room, even in the sheets. His cock hardened and he grunted. Pulling the covers off, he stomped back into the bathroom and sighed.

Just shake this off in the shower, maybe it's the cherry tobacco getting me all aroused again.

A shiver shook his shoulders. He wanted to taste her one more time, feel her fingers reach between them... another grunt escaped him. The lustful want building in him goaded him to turn the shower on once more. Drowning his head in the water, his skin crawled. Biting his lip, his hand slid down, gripping his hardened shaft. He stroked, slow at first as his eyes squeezed shut. He could feel the haunting heat of her body.

The way her eyes glowed and face flushed. And when she dipped her fingers to play with herself with my...

Stroking faster and firmer, he released with a moan. His heart pounded as he watched his cum slide down the drain. He searched the air a moment, chasing the fleeting thoughts that tried to bring calm to the growing desire boiling at his core. Jane couldn't be far.

Small town, gardener of the local B&B... Maybe she ran to the little convenience store across the street?

Armed with that thought, he turned off the shower and began toweling off in a rush. He had to find her, just spend another moment with her. Whether this was long term or just for the weekend, it was worth the chase. Sniffing a shirt, he frowned and searched for a different one. He had been so lost in bitter thoughts about Karen he hadn't bothered to check if everything he shoved in the duffle bag had been clean. Pulling one leg, then the other through a pair of cargo shorts, he almost didn't circle back to slid on his flipflops.

Aiming for the exit, he paused and turned to the manager reading his book. "Hey, where's the gardener."

"Gone," he drawled.

"No, I meant the lady in blue."

He peeked over his book and arched an eyebrow. "Funny. That's a cute one. Though I was thinking the same thing."

"Same thing?" Mark could feel a chill snaking up his back, his gut twisting.

"How long has this place been without a gardener?" Mark's mouth ran dry as he dared to ask the question.

"A few months." Sitting the book down, he stifled a yawn before revealing more information. "But its painfully obvious someone has been keeping the garden in shape. I swear, it hasn't been me or the maid. They say the previous owner hasn't left this place since it opened in the late 1880's."

"The lady in blue..." Mark looked at the man, dead-panned. "Jane."

"Yeah, see you know the history. Jane Story is known to leave behind the smell of..."

"Cherry Tobacco."

"There. You got all the information you need." He grabbed up the book and cracked it open. "I keep smelling it today, she's rather active. If you're lucky, you might see her again." He laughed.

"I think I did more than that," muttered Mark, paling as he covered his mouth.

"What was that?" he broke from the book again.

"Never mind."

Mark wondered out of the B&B, lost in thought as he walked to the convenience store. Without making eye contact or a single sound, he pulled a 24-pack of beer from the wall cooler and marched to the counter. His eyes fell out of focus, his mind choking on disbelief as he tried to digest what or who he had been smitten with.

Could it just be a local hot chick playing the part? I mean, I had sex with her. Didn't I? Am I even awake?

"Hey, I said it's $27.99." The cashier chewed on her bubblegum, popping a bubble. "And I need your ID still."

"R-right." Blinking, he handed her his license and credit card. "Does a girl by the name of Jane live in town?"

"No." Then she smirked. "Except for the ghost in the B&B. Why?"

He shook his head, the information only securing his fears.

"Is this everything?" she asked as she smacked her chewing gum, mouth opened.

Someone should let her know how unattractive that is. He glanced at the wall of tobacco products and he tilted his head, "You got any cherry flavored cigarillos?"

She folded her brow at him. "Like what my Aunt Kathy smokes?" Reaching under the counter, she produced a box of cherry flavored mini cigars. "These?"

Clearing his throat, Mark could feel the heat in his cheeks, "Yeah, those."

She giggled as she rung them up. "You smoke these?"

He narrowed his eyes, "What if I do."

Shrugging, she grinned. "Just seems odd. Unmanly."

"Well, when you grow up and stop chewing gum like a five year old, call me up."

There was silence. She closed her mouth, leaned over and spit her gum in the trash can. "You want my number? I'm ready, big boy."

"Next time, sweetheart." He winked at her, loving her acute response to his snarky comment.

"Come see me when you're back in town, the name's Sam." With that, she slid his license and card back to him.

"Depends if I settle for Jane first," and Mark stomped off with his bagged purchase.

If I can figure out if she's a ghost or a person or... it can't be.

His heart beat hard against his chest, the idea that Jane was a phantom. Other questions crept forward, and he gripped the bag tighter as he crossed the empty street.

Could there be something different about me to make... now I'm just thinking like a b-rated movie. Might as well be the plotline to a bad paranormal themed porno. All it needs is a pizza delivery boy.

Shoulders shuddering, the streetlamps began to flicker to life, exposing how barren of life the town was for a Saturday night. Still, he couldn't shake the doubts and wonderings. His gut twisted every time he circled back to words like *ghost, phantom, or dead.*

Did I have a mental break? Maybe she gave me a false name? No, that's not it.

He paused at the gate, swallowing as something deep inside shook his core.

The door never closed and opened. Not once. There's only one set of stairs up and she wouldn't have made it pass me. It's a tight fit in that foyer. And if that's the case then...

Bushes beside the B&B shook and out came Jane. His heart skipped a beat and again he swallowed. She froze, their eyes meeting. Every fiber in his body wanted her, wanted to drag her back through those bushes and...

Dammit, I must know who she is before I proceed further!

Pushing through the gate, he headed for the front porch steps of the B&B. He broke their stare, choosing to ignore her. Sitting down, he riffled through the bag, ripping the cardboard open and pulling a bottle out. Twisting the cap off, he chucked it to the ground and began guzzling. Jane walked up, reaching down to retrieve it with an annoyed expression.

"I'd appreciate it if you wouldn't throw your trash everywhere." His expression made her blink and she frowned. "C-can I sit with you?"

Shit, she knows something's up.

He slid over, unsure if he should speak. Reaching into the cardboard, he pulled out a beer. Holding it to her, he felt like someone might see him and think he was trying to drink with his imaginary friend. Relief washed over him when she took it from him and popped the cap. She chucked both caps into his bag and he guzzled down the rest of his beer. Without so much as glancing at her, heart racing, he popped the top on another.

"From the way you're acting, I suppose you've figured out who I am." She took a sip, her eyes demanding he look at her and he refused. "Or is the thought more of a what am I?"

"How..." He lost his words. *I can't just say, 'How is it possible to fuck a ghost' can I?*

"When you touched my arm, that was my first thought, *how*." Tilting her head, she took another sip and continued. "Then you offered to have sex and all I could think was how long it had been since the last time I felt the warmth of another human being. Sure, I can feel the heat of the sun and the cold of snow, but what good is that if I'm... well, you can imagine having so many pass through me like I'm made of air, and here you come like it was nothing."

His chest stung. "So you're really her, the Lady in Blue."

"Y-yeah."

He downed his beer, then opened another. *Fuck me. I'm in over my head.*

"I'm sorry, you were just looking for some fun and..." her voice faltered, she finished her beer and reached over him for a second.

Her breast slid over his thighs and he became hard. Cursing under his breath, she paused. There was something electric about thinking of her but feeling her against him brought out a side of him he didn't even know existed. The chemistry in their touch was off the charts and he knew she could feel it, beyond just the dick poking into her tits. There was this hunger for companionship and lust that resonated between them. She pulled away with her beer and smiled to herself.

"Look, Mark. If you want to fool around, I'm game. You're the only man I can do that with anyhow." The beer hissed as it opened, and the cap landed in the cardboard. "You are welcome to hit me up anytime. Plus, your girlfriend is a piece of shit."

"You? You took the picture of Karen?" She sighed, satisfied to finally have his eyes meet hers. "Of course, you did."

"I just found it annoying. Seems like she was sleeping around on you... a lot."

"It always happens that way..." He shifted forward, leaning on his knees, a weak attempt to hide the tent in his shorts. "Every girlfriend I've had has either left me or cheated on me. I swear it's the sex, but..."

"It is," Jane intercepted. "That and well, the other thing..."

He narrowed his eyes. "What other thing? What about the sex? What the hell am I doing wrong?"

What did I miss? Is there something wrong with me? This whole time was it really something wrong with me?

9

Bring Me to Life

Jane faltered from taking a sip of her beer, nearly spewing it. Mark's pitiful expression told her volumes of heartbreak and guilt, as if he had failed his previous loves in the bedroom department. After what little she had in her previous life, he had been leagues better than her belated husband and far outclassed the racy gossip she had heard. In fact, she had been rotten, playing with herself watching the living have intercourse for some sort of release. Regardless, his face said he had convinced himself he was the failure in the sheets, not them.

Poor guy!

Just the flashback of the way he had made love to her hours ago made her shift. A flush of arousal hit her, and she prayed the heat in her face didn't make her cheeks red. The sky was a deep lavender, the moths tinging off the porch light from above. In the yellow lighting, Mark seemed worn down.

What on earth went wrong? she wondered.

She scowled and remembered what the pukwudgie had said, *he doesn't know.* Finishing her beer, she inhaled a deep breath.

Ask him about his dad.

Jane's lips twisted, hesitant to follow a trickster's advice, but they don't befriend and not eat a human often. She had only run into a few of them in passing, marveled the insight and mischief they caused the B&B, a resident, or even the whole damn town. Regardless, some part of her felt keeping something like this secret from someone was right-down wrong.

I just wanted to feel alive in his arms one more time, but I can't shake the feeling this is important. Why can I feel him as if we are on the same physical plane.

"Tell me about your dad," she demanded.

His eyes widened. "Why?"

"Let's just say a little gremlin said I'd know the answer if I asked."

"Why would you want to know?" His face tensed, his eyes darkening. "What answer are you looking for?"

"Why this is possible..." She ran her hand over his bicep and down his arm but jerked back before clasping her fingers into his. "So, tell me something unusual about your parents."

He started to open a pack of cigarillos.

"That bad?"

"He died before I was born." Pulling one free, he flustered. "Dammit, I didn't get any matches or a lighter."

"Here." She flicked a match against the porch and handed it to him. "What's that? It smells a little sweeter than what I've been putting in my pipe. Is that a cigarette? Cigar?"

"Something in between. It's called a cigarillo and they come in a lot of flavors. Try one," he handed her the pack and billowed smoke out. "So, Mom tells this story about my dad. Everyone reassured me it was just a story, but Mom swears it happened and I can't say she's ever been one for ghost stories."

"Ghost story?" She pulled his cigarillo from his lips and used it to light her own before placing it back. "Go on."

"They say he died in the plane crash, but my mom swears by her Bible he came home at the time the black box says the crash happened." He took another drag, the scent of the smoke like the cherry tobacco from her pipe. Strangely, it calmed him. "He didn't say a word. Wouldn't answer her when she asked why he abandoned his flight so suddenly. He just kissed her, made passionate love to her until he uttered her name at last. When she woke up, he was gone, so gone, she said he didn't even leave the usual indentation of his body in the sheets and pillow. Like his spirit laid with her one last time before passing from this world, to do what they had been trying to do in three years of marriage. She swears that's when she got pregnant but... anyway, it's just a... or I thought it... then if... if... never mind."

Jane leaned on her knees, holding her head in disbelief. "It was a wraith."

"W-what did you say?" He leaned into her view and nudged her knee. "It's just a ghost story, you should be used to those by now."

Mark choked on his beer. "You're half wraith," he said, collecting himself.

"Um, what?" he repeated, to breathe. "I'm a what?"

"Wraith. Look, there's old stories about the Co-walker, the doppelganger showing itself when your life is to end and fulfilling one last wish." She downed a beer, then motioned for another.

He paled. "My mom, that night, it wasn't dad but... a doppelganger."

Swallowing the beer, she sputtered, "Right. A type of wraith or banshee. You're not completely human, and you're not completely corporeal because of it."

"I'm not drunk enough for this shit." Mark started to drink faster, his heart racing.

"Look, wraith's often feed off of human life or energy. The more powerful, the more likely they can take on a new corporeal form when the adjacent spirit dies, or it sucks them dry. Let me ask this, do all your sex partners pass out during or after sexual contact?"

He snorted his beer out and dropped his cigarillo down the steps.

"That's part of it but with me..." She looked away, face flushing as she took a long drag off her cigarillo. "You can't suck me dry, and I am more likely to do that to you if I'm not paying attention."

He stood, stomping the cigarillo out and glared at her. "Then why do you have a physical form near me?"

Blowing out a long stream of smoke, she shrugged. "Maybe it's because you're not dead? You provide a link between the dead and living?"

"Wouldn't this happen sooner to me?" Despair filled his face.

"Like a ghost would tell you what they are."

He leaned over her, nose to nose. "Were you planning to tell me?"

Jane's heart raced. She had thought to tell him, maybe at the end of the fun weekend. Her eyes fell to his lips lingering so close. Sweet cherry smoke filled the air, his hard cock pressing against her knee through his shorts, making her wet for him. Caving to the arousal, she pressed her lips against his. He deepened the kiss, the force of it making her abandon and snuff out her cigarillo on the porch beside them.

I wanted to have you think of me as alive a little longer in fear I couldn't have another moment like this.

The bitter taste of cheap beer and cherry tobacco filled her senses. She wanted more of it, more of him. His tongue dipped into her mouth and she suckled it, making it stay. Her knees parted as she laid back onto the porch, moaning as the tent in his pants rubbed against the crotch of her shorts. Wrapping her arms around him, she pulled him closer. The heat of his hand slid under her crop top and she responded with lashing her tongue into his mouth where he, captured it, sucking on it.

His fingers weaseled under the cup of her bra, squeezing her breast tight. Her heart fluttered as she felt him throb where their hips pressed tight. Breaking away, he sucked and nipped on her neck and she arched into him. The heat of his body made her own warm, the rush of life filling her like nothing had ever done before. His breath hot against her skin made her own pimple and she reached down to grope his ass.

He moaned into her neck. "I want to take you over and over again."

A wave of arousal made her shudder. "And I will let you have your way with me over and over again."

His tongue ran up her neck until his lips captured her earlobe. Another wave of goosebumps rolled over her and his cock throbbed. Fingers pinched her nipple and she ached to have his hardened length back inside her. The provocative want for his skin against her own made her whole being buzz with desire. Her hand slipped under his shorts, and grinned to feel he had gone commando to come looking for her. Again, she squeezed his ass cheek and his dick throbbed against her pussy.

Damn these clothes!

"Fuck me right here," she purred in lust.

He nuzzled her ear. "What if they see us?"

"No one comes around on Saturday." She slipped her other hand into the back of his shorts, grinding into his cock and earning a grunt from him. "I bet you can come twice before we're caught."

Mark giggled and she tensed against his stubble chin. "They might just see me with a hardon humping the porch."

"Shit." The color drained from her face and she pulled her hands out. "I'm sorry I didn't think about the fact–"

"Mr. Wilder." The manager's voice made Jane's blood run cold, staring at him wide-eyed where they froze in their embrace. "Not that it's my business what you and this young lady intend to do, but please take it to the privacy of your room upstairs. Small towns frown upon such public displays of affection."

Did he... did he imply he can see me! What the hell is happening?

10

Taking It Slow

"**Y**-yes sir." Mark shot a glance in her direction and they scrambled to their feet. "I meant to tell you; Jane will be staying the night. Not sure if that's an extra charge or..."

"Of course not." Tapping the book on his leg, looking at her, confused. "Jane?" The man was tall, his goatee only made his mouth sterner and the glasses obscured his expression completely from where Mark stood. "Is that really your name, girl in blue?"

"Y-Yes." She looked to Mark, then to the manager, both wondering if the manager could even hear her.

His brow folded and he scratched his jaw in thought.

"I'm local?" Jane cringed, not confident in her focus. "That's right, Mr. Buckley, I just wanted to surprise my boyfriend this weekend." Shuffling over, she hooked an arm with Mark's and picked up the bag of beer. "He's been gone to college and said he was returning home so we rented the Blue Lady room."

"R-right." Now the manager squinted his eyes at them in suspicion. "And that's why the room was registered under his friend's name?"

"About that..." Mark mentally grasped for everything, anything to patch the story they crafted. "I didn't want her to catch on to me coming for a surprise visit."

"Right!" Jane nodded, following his lead. "And well, he didn't know I've been gone. Dealing with..." She inhaled sharply.

Shit, she hit a dead end. Come on, come on, think!

"Taking care of family property." Mark shrugged.

"Yes! That's right."

He chuckled. "Just get upstairs with this before old Aunt May across the street calls me or the sheriff." He shook his head, "You don't have to explain shit to me, just don't trash the room like last weekend's couple."

Mark flinched, but Jane pinched him in the ribs. "Ouch. Why'd you do that for?"

"You heard the man. Upstairs. Now. Before anyone *sees,*" she hissed, tugging him into the room.

The door shut behind her and she leaned against it. Mark held his head, both staring at one another in shock. He managed to motion to her and couldn't find the words. She lipped *I know!* Blue eyes wide and chest rising and falling with her quickened breath. Mark looked to the ceiling, still holding his head in disbelief.

Is that what I can do? Make ghost flesh for a fleeting moment?

A rush of heat pressed hard against him. Jane had buried herself into his chest. Arms wrapping him tight, fists balling his shirt as she clung to him. Blinking, registering what was happening, he wrapped his own around her. She was crying, sobbing into him. He rested a cheek on the top of her head, sighing as he let her carry on.

And to be dead, haunting your home for this long. What does this mean if I leave her? Does she go back to that life? Back to an afterlife of barely existing.

His chest burned, swallowing the fear rattling him at his core. "Will you be okay?" He spoke in a soft voice soft as he held her tight.

Catching her breath, she at last answered, "I'll deal, I've gone this long but..."

"But?" She released him at last and he wiped a tear.

Holding his hand there, her eyes glowed and took his breath away. "Would it be too wrong to ask that you visit again? To let me feel alive for a night or day?"

"That's a hard thing to promise." It broke him to say it, but they both needed to assess the situation. "So, I could see you and hear you. There's so much to digest. It's amazing, he could hear and see you."

She laughed, "I swear he's been doing that the whole time. That man comes out to the porch and talks to me all the time."

Mark snorted. "From what I hear, you've made a lot of folks very aware you were here long before I made this happen."

"How are you doing it?" She sniffled and he shrugged.

"Honestly? I have no idea."

"I suppose you should ask Tim." She puffed out her cheeks.

"Tim? My friend Tim?" His mind spiraled. "Why would he know anything?"

"He's a pukwudgie with a PhD." Mark's face must have revealed his mind was spinning circles to nowhere. "Oh no, you didn't know? You really don't know anything at all." Puffing out her cheeks once more, she flustered, "Dammit. He's just causing havoc, that little twerp."

Mark smirked, seeing that flare of anger and annoyance she had given him that first moment he had touched her. He kissed her, hands gliding back under her shirt. This time his hand drifted to her back and unlatched the bra, again, with speed and accuracy. She inhaled, a shiver making her shake against him. Breaking away, he lifted her shirt and bra off eager to see her naked before him, hungry to touch and taste her. A grin grew on her face and she reached down and began to unbutton his shorts. Tugging off his own shirt, he moaned as the heat of her fingers wrapped around his cock.

Which way do I want to take her first? She's been dead, she can feel for the first time in ages... I can take it slow, make sure I keep myself teetering on the edge.

Tilting his hip, he pressed his cock into her palm, and she tightened her grip, stroking firmer. Tracing her cheek with his finger, he looked at her with endearment. They flowed over the pronounced collarbone and between her subtle breasts. Her skin pimpled, pink nipples erect as he travelled down the center of her torso. A sharp inhale escaped her lips, the stroking fingers on his dick halting.

To think, this gorgeous woman is dead, watching life come and go for centuries. I get her all to myself, mine, and mine alone. Someone to enjoy endless...

His fingers stopped at the waistband and he frowned. "These are in the way."

"Then remove them," she challenged.

Biting his bottom lip, he was slow with the way he unbuttoned her shorts. "So, tell me, how does a late 1800's ghost end up in a pair of daisy dukes?"

She abandoned her play and buried her face in his bare chest. "I learned really fast that I could materialize my favorite items, so I thought maybe I could mimic things I saw."

"And you chose this?" He unzipped her shorts, slow as he felt each notch unhook.

"If you don't like it, then take it off me."

His eyes locked with hers as she looked up. "Can't a guy enjoy a hot chick undressing for just a minute or two?"

She laughed and it made his heart flutter. Her hands slipped over his hip, shoving his own pants down and they fell to the floor. Arching his eyebrows high, the zipper finally couldn't travel any further. The room grew dark, casting deep shadows over their bodies as the last of her own clothes joined his at their feet. Kissing her, he groped her ass, walking her backwards until her knees locked on the bed. She fell back and his hands raced up her thighs, parting them as he kneeled on the floor.

I want to make her scream like a banshee... everyone will know her voice by the time I finish with her tonight. Jane Story will be heard by the entire town by the time I'm done with her.

Running his tongue across her pussy and ending with a flick to her clit. She moaned, legs shaking as she fought to close them around him. Again, he licked the length of her opening, tasting her until he wrapped his lips around the swollen jewel. Suckling, he slipped a finger inside her wet heat, and she arched, knees raising until her legs rested on either shoulder. Mark moaned and felt her tighten around his finger. A second digit joined, and he stroked her slow.

The jittering in her legs told him that at last, with a twist of his wrist, he had found a sweet spot for his fingers to rub. Sucking more aggressive on her clit, locking it in his lips, he flicked it with the tip of his tongue. She squealed, her pussy squeezing on his fingers. He stroked hard and fast, focusing on the spot that had made her body jolt. A visceral scream exploded from her. Back arching, heels digging into his backside as her thighs threatened to clamp shut around him.

That's the scream I was looking for. Good girl. Keep howling. Let them hear you!

Leaning back, he shook her legs off, elbows pushing her thighs apart once more. He rubbed her clit his fingers, still stroking her hard and heavy. Another wail and a gush of hot fluid rushed from her pussy. A fountain of ecstasy escaped her and he at last looked up to her sparkling blue eyes. They were wide with surprise, cheeks red as her hands rushed down to pull him from his fun.

"First time coming that hard?" He slowed his thrusting fingers until he pulled them from her throbbing pussy.

"Y-yes," she panted.

"Let's see how many more times I can get you there again."

Before she could refuse, his tongue slide over her swollen pussy and she inhaled sharp. Fingers clenched the hair on his head, but he paid no heed to them. She tasted so sweet, the way her body flinched and shook, shooting waves of stimulating sensations through her whole being. His cock throbbed with want, but he pushed the aching aside, focusing on the task before him.

I want her to beg me to stop or ask me for more...

11

Put on Your Blue Light

Jane's body buzzed in new ways. The hot silk of Mark's tongue slipped between her folds and she sat up, threatening to fold atop him. She had never gushed during an orgasm and now, he lapped it up like a man desperate to satisfy his thirst. Moaning, her fingers tangled in his hair. Arms wrapped around her hips, his hands pulling her pussy into his hungry jowls. She lost herself to the erotic pulses. Her hips rocked and his tongue dove deeper, wiggling inside her. Her breath caught as he slipped in and out before sucking on her clit once more.

To think this man just made me orgasm with his mouth! MERCY ME!

Teeth teased the swollen flesh, bringing on a new level of pleasure. Now she tried to remove him from her thighs. He became more voracious, a hand dropping over her hip and across her inner thigh. Lips wrapped tight, sucking hard on her jewel. Two fingers slid into her dripping folds and rubbed her slow and with purpose once more. They changed location repeatedly until her body betrayed her all over again, flinching the moment he rolled his stroking fingers over a sweet spot. Teeth nibbled at her clit and he rubbed and thrusted in and out. She wailed.

He's going to eat me alive and I want him to devour everything in his path!

Arching back into the bed, she had given up pulling him from her. The orgasm unfolding both inside her pulsing pussy and captivated clit made her muscles tense and legs rattle. Another hot gush escaped her, and he pulled his fingers from her. Rocking back on his heels, she felt his eyes taking in his handiwork, proud and triumphant. An enthralling shiver rolled through her. Never had she orgasmed so deeply, so wholly.

He's fucking me, body and soul like I've never felt when even alive!

Mark didn't stay there long, tasting and kissing his way up the center of her body. She ached for him to latch onto her nipple, but he denied her. Nuzzling at her neck, the tip of his cock rubbing against her opening. Her pussy throbbed and ached to have him inside her. Flashes of the shower making her impatient. Reaching down for his cock, he stopped her. Strong hands gripping her wrists, flinging her back onto the bed, arms pinned under his hands.

"I didn't give you permission to touch that," his voice grumbled, and chills rattled her.

"Oh?" She grinned, excitement building through her as her heart raced. "Since when did I need permission? I didn't need it a moment ago?"

"I'm not done playing with you."

She swallowed, her mouth running dry as his body towered over her. The hardened length of his cock rubbing against her pussy, her thighs hot with the heat of his torso. Her eyes lingered on his lips, marveling over how they had pleased her and how badly she wanted to taste herself on his tongue.

Was I that delicious to you?

"Kiss me," she whispered.

He pressed his lips against hers and the tip of his cock gliding inside her. She moaned, tilting her hips, wanting more of his dick inside. Deepening his kiss, his body weighed heavy against hers. Nipples hard against the hard planes of his torso, she arched into him. His grip on her wrists tightened. She lashed her tongue into his mouth, chasing him. His cock thrusted slow inside her and she moaned with want.

Pulling away, he searched her face. "So, in your time was missionary the only known position?"

She arched an eyebrow. "It's all mine gave me, not everyone was a–" She squeaked, a quick thrust coming from him made her tighten on the throbbing dick inside her.

"Was a what?" Mark smirked, aiming to make her suffer.

"You're being mean." She tightened around his throbbing cock.

"Now, you're being mean." He completely pulled out, leaning into her ear, his voice low, "Did anyone ever make you feel this good?"

Slow and agonizing, the rock-hard cock slid in until their hips pressed tight against one another. He throbbed inside her and she squeezed her pussy around him. Eyes locked, he began rocking against her, grinding in and out. She mimicked the motion, deepening the sensation, frustrated to have her hands pressed firm on the mattress.

"You really like feeling where I enter your pussy, don't you?" His smirk sent her heart fluttering.

"What if I do?" Her arms wiggled and she couldn't break free. "Please...let me feel you."

"I can't," he pressed hard against her, throbbing inside her wet heat.

"Why not?" She continued to rock against him, verging on another orgasm.

"It'll make me want to come before I'm done playing." Another playful jump of his cock. "It's hard enough with as tight as you get."

"Like this?" She squeezed her pussy around his dick, grinding slow.

His head fell in defeat. "But I want you to come for me in missionary."

"Why?" She laughed.

His eyes met hers. "So I can prove I'm better at it."

She looked at him, baffled and astonished for a moment in the darkness of the room. Inhaling deep, she held his words there in her mind, weighing her own emotions.

He means that. He's thought about my situation and intends to give me everything he has to offer.

Hooking her feet together behind him brought his hip tight against hers. He leaned in, the heat of his body against hers, wrists aching under the stress of him atop her. Arching her body, her nipples slid over his muscled chest and both of them shuddered, enthralled with the sensation.

"Then fuck me harder," she demanded.

"You really want it rough, don't you?" He released her wrists, his hands trailing down her arms and over her breasts and torso as he stood tall. "Shouldn't we make a safe word?"

"Why?" Her hands groped her own breasts, licking her lips. "I'm dead, remember?"

"I don't think you understand." He grinded against her, his cock hard inside her throbbing heat as he leaned down to her ear. "You might beg me to stop. This won't be gentle like before."

"Prove it," she hissed back.

"The safe word is," he suckled her ear before rumbling, "cherry."

She laughed. "Fine. Cherry if I can't take anymore, huh?"

"That's right," again the sliding of hands crossed the length of her body making her shudder and tighten her pussy. "I got into a lot of BDSM in hopes I could keep my partners awake, but as you know, that wasn't the issue so, I'm looking forward to breaking you in."

"You make it sound like a conquest." He took a step back, studying her body laying across the bed. "What's wrong?"

"Absolutely nothing." He flicked his finger, signaling she turn around. "I want to take you from behind, you seemed to enjoy that earlier. We'll start there, instead."

"Start there?" Scooting to the edge of the bed, she stood and kissed him.

He deepened it, parting her lips with his own, moaning as the heat of her hands glided over his ribs, flowing down the divot of his spine to grope his ass. His hardened length throbbed between their bodies. Her tongue licked the length of his own and he lashed out. Wrapping and twisting, tasting one another and the subtle hint of cherry tobacco still lingering in one another's mouth. Jane arched into him, her breasts pressing into him making his hunger to fuck her tantalizing as he shuddered. Breaking the kiss, he gripped her shoulders and twisted her in position.

Leaning back into him, she reached down and held his cock against her opening. Heart racing, anxious to see what he had in mind for her next. With new aggression, Mark's arms wrapped around her, an arm angling up to grasp her throat. She stiffened and he knew he had her attention. Her pulse quickened, breath catching. The rock-hard heat of his forearm made it clear he wouldn't allow her to go anywhere. His other hand groped her breast, twisting her nipple hard. She tried to whimper but the slight tightening of his hand on her throat silenced her.

"Good girl." The provocative sound of his voice only matched the way he fondled her breast.

How exciting to feel him get rough... I want more, more of this dominating...

She slowed her breathing, submitting to him and the new-found roughness. Letting go, he moved forward with reassured confidence. Shoving her down onto the bed, he pulled her arms behind her. With a single grip, he bound them behind the small of her back. A slap against an ass cheek made her flinch, his handprint leaving a blossom of red as it surfaced on her skin. Again and again, switching ass cheeks every so often, he smacked her until she no longer flinched and whimpered. The heat of the rushing blood made her sense of touch heighten.

My body nervous, unsure when his touch will be rough and soft. I can't stand it...

His cock teased the opening of her pussy. Her wetness growing with each step of gaining dominance over her. So much so, her thighs had become wet, making the grinding, and rubbing between her legs add to her ache for him to enter her. Mark adjusted his grip on her bound arms pressing down on her as his other hand gripped the nape of her neck. Pulsing his grasp from tight to lose, her breath quickening and he shuddered with excitement.

"Please... fuck me..." she whimpered.

I have never wanted a cock inside me so desperately in all my years on this earth!

12

Call Me Daddy

Mark didn't even react as the blue lamp flickered to life. The blue ambience only added to the mood, the curves of her body mesmerizing in the color. His cock throbbed against her hot, wet pussy. He wanted to take her, but that was the hardest part of playing the dominate one. Deep down he cursed himself for not bringing any of the toys, a satchel filled with vibrators, cuffs, nipple clamps, and more. It had been abandoned under his bed, haunting him and now, he had found someone to play with him.

I wonder if I can make her scream cherry without them?

Licking his lip, he pressed his weight into her, teasing her with the idea he might enter her at any moment. She whimpered in hushed tones, pleading for him to fuck her. Releasing the back of her neck, he towered over her. Spanking her over and over again, her grinding against his cock telling him how desperately she wanted him inside her. The blue light caught a trickle of her juice rundown her leg. She had only gotten wetter with each move he made.

She's very into this. I don't think I've ever seen a girl get this wet at this stage of the dominance.

"Mark, fuck me, please." She tried the push back into him and he held her in place by her arms. "Please, I can't take it anymore–"

His arm scooped under her, making her arch as his powerful forearm slide between her breasts. Fingers wrapped around her throat and muffled her words. A shudder rattled her, and he could tell she was excited. He didn't make it impossible for her to talk, no he still wanted to hear her scream after all and wanted to satisfaction to hear her utter *cherry*. He nuzzled into her neck and shoulder, sucking hard and nibbling at her like some predator. She tasted sweet and salty on his tongue. As he played and teased her, he waited for the calm to hit her breathing and pulse. The high and lows of adrenaline were his favorite to toy with.

"Beg me some more," his voice rumbled, and his cock throbbed.

"Punish me."

He smirked; *she's catching on*.

"Please, punish me," she breathed. "Show me how bad I've been."

"Wasn't your spanking enough?" He caught her earlobe between his teeth, then whispered, "I loved your dessert." His cock rubbed across her opening. "Beg Daddy for more. Tell me what you want me to do with this."

"Fill me up until I burst, please, Daddy." The weight of desire in her voice proved more than he could resist.

Tilting his hips, the tip of his cock entered her pussy. Her body was on fire, he had worked her up to a breaking point. Arching her body, one hand locking her arms behind her while the other still held her throat. Pushing deep inside her, he took his time as she tensed and relaxed, like her pussy gobbling up his dick. She was soaking wet, whimpering as he rode through her. At last he couldn't push himself any deeper, biting at her neck like he threatened to devour her on every level her body could provide him. She tried to speak, and he threatened to tighten his fingers.

In the window, he caught their reflection. They looked like phantoms with the way the blue light hit them. Two creatures feeling corporeal for the first time in their ghostly presence. One invisible, the other denied the ecstasy of connecting with the living in the way he ensnared her. Her eyes glowed, and he blinked for a moment. Even his own shared the eerie glow of something more.

Half wraith... feeding on the living... but with her... I feel... complete.

Rocking his hips, thrusting his cock in and out of her swollen folds she moaned. He loved how wet she grew with each stroke. She tightened, soaking the front of his thighs with her juices. His balls ached with the need for release, but he fought it back. There was still much work to do but the temptation to let himself cum inside her once more never left the back of his mind. Thoughts crept back to the shower and he grunted, tightening his hold on her.

I can't stand it; I can't hold back. I want to take her. After this, I should be able to hold out longer... I'm going to have to cave.

Releasing her throat, he let her bend over, face against the bed. Now he gripped her arms with both hands like fleshy guard rails. Pressing deep inside her, he waited, gauging her body a moment. Goosebumps rippled across her skin, shimmering in the blue light of the lamp. Biting his bottom lip, he prepared himself for the next move. Pushing his weight on her arms and hips, he began thrusting hard and fast, like a racehorse fresh out of the gate. He couldn't hold the rapid succession thrusting for long, but she had been more than primed to orgasm.

A scream erupted from her. He didn't slow, pounding her as her pussy tightened. The smacking of their bodies filling his ears and driving him forward. His grip tightened, his cock hardening as he teetered on the edge of his own orgasm. Exhaling, he moaned as he released inside her, push hard against her to fill her in her deepest depths. Her shrieking shifted to heavy panting, sweat painting both their bodies from the rapid grinding he had given her.

Releasing her arms, he grabbed her ass cheeks, spreading her so he could watch his dick slide, in and out of her swollen pussy. At last, the tip came free and he smirked, watching his cum drizzle out of her. He rubbed his cock's tip in the sticky liquid and shoved it back into her heat with force. She yelped, tightening. He wasn't nowhere as hard before, but he loved the state he had broken her into. Every touch he gave her would set her back to near peak. Her pussy throbbed and he pulled out, more cum sliding from between her folds before using his cock to force it back into her. Another shriek and her body gushed.

He met her eyes in the window's reflection and smiled. "Well?"

"I thought..." She hummed as he grinded slow against her.

"You thought?"

Inhaling deep, she tried to speak again, "You were going to rip me apart with your dick, or I'd catch fire from the speed you pounded it into me."

"Maybe I was trying to start a fire." His eyes fell to her ass, watching as his cock slid out and this time, he let his cum escape, dripping down between her thighs.

"Like what you see?" She grinned when he met her reflection again.

"I like everything about you, Jane." His hand slid down over her pussy, making them slick from their juices as he rode between her folds until he found the hard nub of flesh. "I suppose I should let you choose what we do next?"

"I want to..." She tensed, fighting back a whimper of pleasure as he rubbed the tender flesh. "I want to sit on top."

"On top? Cowgirl position?" He arched a brow and stepped back. "If that's what you want."

She rolled over, standing to her feet with a bashful expression. "B-but I've never done it. I just... watched."

Mark laughed. "We're breaking a lot of firsts for you today, aren't we?"

"Well, fucking me from behind is a new favorite. What's that position called? Do they all have such ironic names?"

"That one's called Doggy style." He laughed at her grimace. "I like it because I can reach all the fun places so..." His eyes glided over her, making her hyper aware he meant breasts and clit. "So you want to have to do something new?"

Her hands glided over his torso, eyes hungry as she gripped his cock and made him moan. "I want to ride on this, please Daddy."

"Oh, how can I say no to that?" He kissed her, then bit her bottom lip before releasing it. "If I let you on top..." He spun them so he could back into the bed. "You have to do every position I want, without a fuss. You promise to be a good girl, for Daddy?"

"T-there's more than one on top position for me to do?" Her eyes widened.

"Oh yeah..." He broke away, laying on the bed stroking himself to stay hard. "Let Daddy teach you. Bad girls should do their homework after all."

"Is this..." Jane straddled his legs, her breathing quickened as her eyes fell to his dick. "Is this also part of my punishment?"

"Oh yeah..." He motioned for her to crawl closer. "That's a good girl, let's get you on the saddle."

"Aren't you tired?" She was close enough to the tip of his cock that it rubbed against her lower belly, precum making her skin slick.

"Not if you're gonna take over." He grabbed her thighs and slid her into place. "Now, be a good girl and guide Daddy's cock inside."

The goosebumps rolling over her made him excited. She had wanted to do this, was starving for a chance to try all the new things only he could offer her. Her body trembled, her hands reaching down between them as she rose to hover over his cock. The expression of helplessness made him throb in her hand and she scowled.

"What next?" she hissed.

"Sit on it." He tilted his hips, his cock slick as it slid in her hand and pressed against her pussy.

"Just sit on it? That's it?"

"No, but that's the first step." Gliding his hands up her body, he squeezed her breasts, massaging them. "Be a good girl and sit for Daddy."

Humming, she guided him into her opening and eased down until she sat on top of him. His cock flinched inside her and she gasped. She looked down at him, smirking.

Oh, she's already into this!

13

Cowgirl Jane

Jane's heart pounded, sitting on him, legs straddled on either side of his torso, his cock inside her as she glared down at him. The pose was provocative and new. His hungry hands gripped her breasts, twisting her nipples. Inside her pussy she could feel his cock throb. She tightened and loosened, fascinated to the new array of pleasurable sensations that invaded her body. Shifting forward some, he slid inside a little more and she inhaled sharply.

"Rock your hips for me."

A shudder rattled her. His voice had become deep and demanding. Everything about it added to the eroticism unfolding between them. She wanted to learn more until she knew how to make him orgasm as easily as he made hers peak. Rocking her hips, she could feel how her body moved his cock inside her, rubbing in several places. She mimicked the way she had seen other girls had done. Her entire torso snaking so she could move his cock in ways to please herself.

It's like fucking myself, but I'm using his cock. Does... does he feel this?

Reaching down, she braced herself on his torso, shifting into a more favorable position as she rocked her hips. Now she had her thighs lifting and dropping her along the length of his cock, wanting to feel him, mimic what he had done and more. She began moaning, enjoying how the way he felt inside her and all under her control. The heat of his hands released her breasts and gripped her hips, rocking in rhythm with her movements.

"Good Girl... ride Daddy until you come."

"Y-yes..." She picked up speed, enjoying how they grinded against one another like a sexual dance. "This feels... this feels..."

"Tell me. Tell me how much you like Daddy's cock inside you." He slid a hand off her hip, a thumb pushing between them and to rub her clit.

Jane jerked upright, leaning back until she braced herself on his thighs.

"I'm sorry, did I ruin your fun?" He smirked.

"N-no." She started to rock again. *This angle is completely different but just as... as...*

Thoughts derailed, the arousal and pleasure consumed every part of her. He continued playing with her clit, the new angle exposing another level of indulgence to her. With each motion, she was coming closer to another orgasm. Her pussy tightened and he pulled away his thumb, making her falter. Looking down at him he laughed at the way she pouted.

"No fair!" Then she paused.

"You can reach, why do I have to do all the work." He had a glint in his eyes, playful as he placed his arms behind his head. "I wanna see the bad girl orgasm from my cock."

Her expression turned serious. With one arm still bracing against his thigh, she slid her hand between them. Her fingers were soaked, making her breath catch at the idea she had been gushing so heavily during everything. At first, she rocked, fingers rubbing where his shaft slid in and out. At last, her fingers trailed up and began circling her clit. Instantly, her legs began to shake, everything already tender. Her gaze met his, both of them serious and intense as she rocked harder. The rising orgasm made her tighten, his cock hardened and throbbed in response.

At last, the orgasm peaked, making her fall forward as she moaned. Before she could finish riding out the peak, his arms wrapped around her. Pressed tightly into him, he pounded her with the burst of speed from before. She wailed, Back arching and arms hard as stone locking her there. Straddled over him, hard cock fucking her fast, she gushed once more. He slowed and let go and she collapsed against him, panting.

"Good girl," he whispered, licking her ear. "Now sit on Daddy's face and eat my cock."

She pulled herself into a sitting position, his cock still hard inside her. "And how can I do both simultaneously?"

He flicked his finger, motioning she turn around. "Turn it around, love. Keep your knees above my shoulder so I can eat you while you suck my cock."

Inhaling deep, her face seemed red even in the blue light. "Is this a favorite of yours?"

Mark twisted his lips and answered, "To be honest, every man on this earth is merciless the moment their dick reaches a girl's mouth."

"Is that so?" She braced against his torso, standing to reveal the wetness between her thigh and legs. "Mercy me. My dam's broke."

He chuckled. "Hurry up. It's cold."

She shushed him, hesitant to kneel above his face. "Are you sure about this?"

"Sit down already."

He gripped her ass cheeks, shoving her down onto him. The ferocity of his lips and tongue against her sensitive pussy had her folding over him, lips lingering close to his hard cock. She griped him stroking and at last wrapped her lips around the tip. He tilted his hip, sliding his shaft a little deeper and she realized she needed to mimic the movements he needed to cum. She began sucking and wiggling her tongue, both of them rocking themselves into each other, wanting more. She managed to have the tip hit the back of her throat and he rewarded her with his tongue inside her, wiggling as they both moaned with the pleasure of it all. Jane enjoyed the tit-for-tat game it became, learning fast what he liked, experimenting with ways to use her tongue, lips, and hands could make him moan into her pussy.

The door opened and Karen stumbled in. Jane deep throated, sucking hard as she fondled his balls. His moaning escalated as she kept the hard suckling going riding her lips up and down his hardened shaft. Cum squirted hot and thick into her mouth, eyes still locked with Karen's. Satisfied he emptied it all into her, she sat up, rocking her hips on his face.

Opening her mouth, cum rolling on her tongue broke the cheating harlot. Swallowing, Jane was starting orgasm again, his tongue inside her flickering and thrusting. Karen snapped a photo and Jane grinned wildly at the idea.

And one more photo for his collection.

"I swallowed it all, Daddy." She couldn't stop moaning, he continued play verging into the unbearable with Karen watching.

Karen's cheeks puff out. At last, she turned and left as Jane shouted her next words.

"Please, punish me. Eat me, teach me, make me to come for you, Daddy, please!"

Mark's hands slid up her torso and groped her breasts. She came hard, again lunging forward. She tried to crawl away, but again strong arms kept her locked into place. Screaming, visceral and wild, she could take it. He wasn't stopping. Lips suckling her clit, everything on fire with overwhelming pleasure. Teeth teased the swollen flesh and–

"CHERRY!"

She inhaled sharp, shocked she had screamed it. He had paused and released her clit. Arms released her and she crawled away some and looked over her shoulder. Mark smiled, propping himself up by his elbows, his face, neck and chest soaked.

Clearing his throat, he tilted his head. "Did you just shout, cherry?"

She twisted around and covered her face.

"Well, I am pretty sure I heard the safe word."

Dropping her hands, she confessed, "I said... cherry."

He collapsed back, covering his face.

"Wh-what's wrong?" She climbed up to him. "You won. You knew I would cave."

This time, he lowered his hands. "For a moment there, during that blowjob, I thought I might have to call it. You had me, I was done for and I put you there."

They started to laugh. After a long silent moment, they took a shower, both sore and exhausted. It didn't take long before the spooned in the covers, falling asleep in the heat of one another's naked bodies.

"Please, tell me this wasn't a dream." He sounded sad.

She sighed. "No, this was no dream," she said. "Just come back to me. Just one more time later in this short life you have."

"Promise..."

And then, he dozed off.

14

Mark Long Lost Girlfriend

Mark woke to the sound of knocking.

"Mr. Wilder, check out time is in an hour."

"Y-yes sir. Showering and checking out," he shouted.

"Very well," and he could hear his steps fade.

Groaning, his body ached from the night long excursion of sex. Part of him felt relieved, as if a knot in his core had been untangled. Perhaps it had been the ability to let go completely on a sexual level for the first time. Sure, he had tried going to an orgy once, thinking he was *broken*. At the end of that experience and picking up some new tricks, he realized he rather be monogamous. The idea to master someone's body, know all their secrets and learn new ways to exploit them got him hot and bothered.

He rolled over and frowned. "Dammit, she's gone again without a trace."

Mark stumbled his way to the shower. Hot water beating on his sore muscles were a warm welcome, his skin still felt sticky and salty from a night of ecstasy, despite the shower they took. He looked down at his flaccid cock and laughed.

I don't think it'll want to see any action for a while...

Drowning his face in the stream of water, flashes of the night rattled through him. At one point, he swore he saw Karen.

In the window, like she walked in on us and took a picture? Couldn't have been... Granted I was a little busy eating pussy to really care after cumming so hard.

Shaking off the thought, he focused on scrubbing faster.

Shit, where's my phone?

He tilted his head, lathering up every inch of skin for good measure.

Man, I can't tell if I'm sticky from sweat, cum, or...her.

Another brazen grin curved his lips as he began rinsing the soap off.

Oh, shit, I didn't think about recording any of last night...

His face grew red at the thought as he cut the water off. "Would she even let me? I mean, it would be for me later and not to post on some site to proclaim *I fucked the Blue Lady.*"

Dressing, he scrambled around gathering what little he brought along. Still no phone. In fact, a lot of the mess they had created was gone as if it all had been an apparition. Even the sheet lacked the large wet stain of when he made her gush not once, but twice before pounding her so mercilessly. Checking in the drawers, under the bed and nightstand, he still couldn't find his phone.

"Maybe she cleaned up to hide the mess?" Scratching his chin, he headed downstairs. "But where the hell is my phone?"

Leaving out the door, he gave the room one last look. *Wonder if I come back if she'll show up again.*

Making his way to the front counter, he slid the key to the manager. "Here you go with just a few minutes to spare."

The man lowered his book and sized him up. "And your lady friend?"

His face flushed. "She left before me."

"You two must've had quite a night." The manager closed his book and smirked. "The *whole* night it seems."

"Sorry for the noise?" Mark didn't know what to say.

"Didn't bother me." He chuckled. "But your girl screamed good and loud that old Aunt May across the street left plenty of voicemails about it. She's got a set of lungs or you're that good."

Mark shrugged. "It's been a while since either of us have hooked up. What can I say?"

"And the town now knows that much." He picked the book up.

"Uh, have you seen a cell phone?" Mark changed topics, already unnerved about the volume in which they had reached. *Careful what I wish for, I suppose. The town indeed heard Jane Story last night.*

"This one?" It was like a magic trick as he pulled the cell phone from thin air. "Found it on the front porch after I shooed you two upstairs."

"Oh, that makes sense." It wouldn't turn on. "Damn, dead battery. Look, do I owe you any more for the stay?"

The manager wouldn't meet his gaze. "None, Mr. Wilder. Do return though, and maybe a little sooner and not later if this is the result of an extended time away."

"R-right." Mark started for the door but paused. "What book are you reading?"

"Bound by Fire," he drawled. "Plucked it from a guest and it's rather good. I suppose I should return it so she can finish writing it."

Mark made a confused expression. "Typically, they write it, then it becomes a book."

"I'm very aware of the fact, Mr. Wilder." He cleared his throat and lowered his voice. "And typically, my guest don't fuck and date the undead."

"Wait, what?" Mark rushed the counter, unsure of the rasping whisper.

"Good day, Mr. Wilder. Give Jane my regards." He spun the chair away, giving Mark the cold shoulder.

Sighing, Mark pushed out to the front porch and paused. A breeze blew pass him and he could smell a hint of cherry tobacco, more along the lines of the cigarillos. He smiled. Even if he couldn't see her, the idea he could leave her with something new to enjoy made him happy. Marching down the walkway, he paused at the gate and took a look back. It seemed odd now, looking where he had seen her gardening on that first day. He hadn't even noticed anything abnormal about her. Part of him ached to see her one more time, say goodbye.

Maybe her time was up? Or could it be she can only show herself during certain times?

Slumping his shoulders, he made his way to his car. Sliding into the driver seat, he tossed the duffle bag into the back and started the engine cranking the air conditioning to high. Plugging in his phone, he started it. In an instant the cell phone came to life with missed texts and voicemails, and most of them were from Karen. Rolling his eyes, he pulled up the chain of texts and paled.

"What the fuck is this?"

There on the screen was a picture of Jane sitting on his face, his cock standing erect, from Karen simply stating:

[Karen: I get it. You wanted to get caught like I did. Thanks. I don't need this bullshit. Enjoy your new whore of a girl-friend, asshole!]

Not a bad shot, her titties are in full focus and that look on her face, oo!

He felt himself get a little hard and scrolled up to see the text someone had sent her. Covering his mouth, he grinned. Karen had been set up and he now knew he *had seen* her in the middle of their fun. Saving the photo of Jane, he flipped to the gallery and his eyes widened.

"Well look at that!" He shifted in his driver seat, heart racing. "Jane was a busy girl. When did she sneak off with my phone to do..." Face red, he thumbed through the collection of racy and seductive photos. "Oh, these are going to keep me busy for a while."

Another text pinged through.

[Timmy: You okay? Figured you'd be heading home by now. Please tell me you're okay?]

[Mark: Yeah. Just got to my car. Phone died.]

[Timmy: Did you have fun? Hook up with someone?]

Mark covered his face pondering whether to say something. At last, he sent a less racy and more seductive photo of Jane. He couldn't hold back showing off someone so beautiful and amazing.

[Mark: The gardener. *Picture*]

[Timmy: Uh... we need to talk about your new girlfriend, buddy.]

[Mark: Well, not exactly girlfriend... I hooked up, not exactly a girl I can take home to mom, even if I wanted to.]

There was a long pause, the writing indicator stopping and starting a few times before at last the text came through.

[Timmy: Did she tell you?]

Mark blinked at the question and it all came flooding back. Jane had said something about Timmy, and how a lot of her own tribulations were his doing. Swallowing, Mark remembered the weird questions he'd received the first night he'd met

Tim at a fraternity party. He dialed the number, waiting for him to pick up.

"Hey, Mark?" Timmy's voice gave nothing away.

"Tim. Is this... is this about my Dad?" His throat and chest tightened with anxiety.

"Yeah, look... I'm not very truthful about who or what I am, but you need help or you..." He halted as if afraid to go too far. "We need to talk face to face. What are the chances you are willing to take a drive with me to Bridgewater Trinity College? Oh, and you're gonna have to bring Jane, I may have made a large miscalculation on how this would affect you."

"What the hell is..." Mark swallowed, his hand on the wheel semi-transparent. "FUCK!"

"The Manager gave me a call and said the two of you have... flipped roles. SURPRISE!" Tim waited, the silence haunting. "Now, go get your poltergeist of a girlfriend and head my way. Stay close together, should keep you both corporeal until we can fix the natural order of things or get you something to help you two through this."

Epilogue

Karen stood outside of the B&B, a little pass midnight. The whole town seemed barren, almost to the point of a ghost town. Upstairs she could see the blue light coming from the window of her aimed destination. Mark awaited for her. A wicked grin crawled across her face. He had taken longer than she expected to make up with her, but this was borderline hot.

Was he jealous and wanted to fuck me here in this cheezy B&B? I knew he'd come around and forgive me. Besides, men don't break it off with me... I break up with them. I'll have fun, but after this he can kiss my ass. About time I go back to finding some fresh meat, someone with more money and can spoil me on occasion. Damn shame that Satch guy at the casino didn't work out last summer. Would have totally broke it off with Mark sooner for a man like that! Man, could he eat a pussy!

A shudder rolled through her, but she pushed down the walkway and up the porch through the entrance. The manager's counter was empty, and she snorted. *Good riddance! That man was an asshole!* Eyeing the stairs, she pulled out her phone and read Mark's text once more.

[Mark: The Blue Lady Room. Midnight.]

Glancing at the clock, it was pushing closer to two in the morning. "Hope I'm not too late."

Besides, I needed him to sweat. Break his heart, revive it, and shatter it later. That's what he gets for breaking up with me over a damn texted picture. So what if I fucked a football player, what does it matter to him whose dick I fuck when I can't stay awake for his!

Gripping her phone tight, she headed to the top floor.

Bringing me back here where I–

Sounds of a couple fucking couple halted her steps.

She paled. *He wouldn't dare! And with who! No way that loser found someone to screw in just under a week's time.*

She rushed to the Blue Lady room door and found it cracked open. Pushing the door open wide, the whole place was lit with the blue light from the lamp on the nightstand. Her eyes fell on a girl choking down a cock. From here she stood, they were locked into the sixty-nine position. The moaning from the man told her he was coming– *no, Mark. That's how Mark sounds when...* She searched the floor, seeing the familiar duffle bag with his last name *Wilder* embroidered into it.

Rage filled Karen, glancing back to the interlocked couple. Jane locked eyes with her, stroking and sucking him, making his orgasm linger a little longer as she rocked her hips on her face. Pulling her lips off his swollen shaft, she cracks her mouth open to show off the cum rolling on her tongue. Karen's eyes widen, shaking with anger and rendered speechless.

Jane swallowed, sitting up, still grinding into his face. "I swallowed it all, Daddy."

Karen's cheeks puff out, her mind spiraling. *That's what I call him in the bedroom, bitch!*

Inhaling deep, Karen raised her phone to threaten to take a picture, as someone had done to her. Mark moaned under the rocking hips. His hands crawling up Jane's body, one groping her breast and the other gripping her neck. Jane's breath caught, as she started to orgasm. Karen snapped the shot, but they didn't slow. Spinning on her heels, she had seen more than what she bargained for.

"Please, punish me." Jane gave Karen a wicked grin. "Eat me, teach me, make me come for you, Daddy, please!"

Spiteful tears rolled down her cheeks as she flew down the stairs and out the door. She pulled up the image, the way the girl stared at her seemed ghostly.

Eyes don't glow like that! Could he really be fucking the Lady in Blue? Fuck this!

She sent a text, ending it for good.

[Karen: I get it. You caught me, now I've caught you. I'm out of your life, enjoy your ghost girl asshole! *Picture*]

[Phillipe: Hey. Booty call?]

[Karen: Fuck you!]

[Phillipe: Um. That's the point.]

Karen throws her phone to the ground, smashing it under her heel.

"This is bullshit!"

The End

Honey Cummings

A passionate, award-winning author of Fantasy, Honey has turned her aim towards erotica. Blending everyday scenarios and crafting them into steamy, blood-boiling moments for every shade of audience. Whether you want something short and hot like a student-teacher hook up to the more paranormal flair where Sleep with Sasquatch has unexpected bonus, look forward to erotic short stories, novellas, and hopefully a Trilogy in the future. Honey's debut erotic short landed No. 3 in Urban Erotica and continues to satisfy readers time and time again. Be sure to leave her a review and let her know what you think!

https://www.amazon.com/Honey-Cummings/e/
B07WFX5FDX
www.AuthorHoneyCummings.com
instagram.com/authorhoneycummings
twitter.com/HoneyCummings2
facebook.com/
Author-Honey-Cummings-101408818012749

MORE HONEY CUMMINGS BOOKS

Sleeping with Sasquatch
Cuddling with Chupacabra
Naked with New Jersey Devil
Laying with the Lady in Blue
Wanton Woman in White
Beating it with Bloody Mary

Beau and Professor Bestialora
The Goat's Gruff
Goldie and Her Three Beards
Pied Piper's Pipe
Princess Pea's Bed
Jack's Beanstalk
Pulling Rapuzel's Hair

4 HORSEMEN PUBLICATIONS EROTICA

DALIA LANCE
My Home on Whore Island
Slumming It on Slut Street
Training of the Tramp

72% Match
It Was Meant To Be... or Whatever

CHASTITY VELDT
Molly in Milwaukee
Irene in Indianaolis

ALI WHIPPE
Office Hours
Tutoring Center
Athletics
Extra Credit

Bound for Release
Fetish Circuit
Sexual Tourist
Now You See Me

LGBT EROTICA

GRAYSON ACE
How I Got Here
First Year Out of the Closet
You're Only a Top?
You're Only a Bottom

LEO SPARX
Claiming Alexander
Taming Alexander
Saving Alexander

4HorsemenPublications.com

www.ingramcontent.com/pod-product-compliance
Lightning Source LLC
Chambersburg PA
CBHW050155110726
47898CB00008B/2810